THE CLASSROOM

When Nature Calls, Hang Up!

THE CLASSROOM

When Nature Calls, Hang Up!

Directed by Robin Mellom

Filmed by Stephen Gilpin

DISNEY • HYPERION
Los Angeles   New York

For all you courageous field trip chaperones . . .
thank you.
—R.M.

For Amos as he passes into teenagerhood—
I wish I had some advice . . .
that you would actually listen to.
—S.G.

Text copyright © 2015 by Robin Mellom
Illustrations copyright © 2015 by Stephen Gilpin

Printed in the United States
First Edition, June 2015
1 3 5 7 9 10 8 6 4 2

G475-5664-5-15091

Library of Congress Cataloging-in-Publication Data

Mellom, Robin, author.

 The Classroom : when nature calls, hang up! / directed by Robin Mellom ; filmed by Stephen Gilpin.— First edition.

      pages cm.—(The Classroom ; bk. 4)

 Summary: The school year is almost over and it is time for Westside Middle School's annual camping trip, something that Trevor Jones would desperately like to get out of as he is terrified at the prospect of coyotes, bears, dining halls, and eighth graders—and his cabin is supposed to be haunted.

  ISBN 978-1-4231-5066-4

1.   School field trips—Juvenile fiction. 2. Camping—Juvenile fiction. 3. Middle schools—Juvenile fiction. 4. Friendship—Juvenile fiction. 5. Documentary films—Production and direction—Juvenile fiction. [1. School field trips—Fiction. 2. Camps—Fiction. 3. Middle schools—Fiction. 4. Schools—Fiction. 5. Friendship—Fiction. 6. Documentary films—Production and direction—Fiction.] I. Gilpin, Stephen, illustrator. II. Title. III. Title: When nature calls, hang up! IV. Series: Mellom, Robin. Classroom ; 4.

  PZ7.M16254Cn 2015

  813.6—dc23   2014028685

Reinforced binding

www.DisneyBooks.com

THE CLASSROOM

When Nature Calls, Hang Up!

>>Production: THE CLASSROOM

Over on Miller Street, behind the brick walls of Westside Middle School, there are desks. There are lockers. There are worksheets, textbooks, pencils, pens, and squeaky hallway floors that are buffed clean every Friday, right around four.

But one day in particular—during the week when all of Westside heads off to Camp Whispering Pines—the floors aren't just buffed . . . they're waxed. Gloriously waxed. And Wilson, the janitor who shall not be called a janitor, looks forward to it every year.

It's pretty much the reason why he took the job.

At Westside Middle School, you will find a vice principal, counselors, lots of teachers, and, of course, students. One of those students is Trevor Jones—your normal, average, slightly neurotic, often embarrassed, usually-slipping-on-something, (but several times) totally epic student.

Trevor Jones fears, however, that "epicness" is not something he will experience on the all-school overnight field trip to Camp Whispering Pines. It might be three days and two nights of utter humiliation.

This documentary crew set out to tell the story of Trevor and his also-sometimes-epic-but-usually-normal classmates as they experience the wild outdoors. With bugs. And dirt. And bears. And dining halls. Not to mention the crisp smell of humiliation.

Westside is their middle school.

And these are their stories.

Wilson

Senior head of
custodial support,
not the janitor

8:25 a.m.

It's my favorite time of the year. This is the last week of school, and tomorrow Westside Middle School will take its end-of-year overnight trip. That means three days and two nights of no students. No teachers. No vice principals.

NO FOOTPRINTS WHATSOEVER.

Just me, an entire school of dirty floors, and one turbocharged floor buffer. But the floors don't just get buffed . . . they get the entire treatment. Yep, it's my one chance during the school year to use hot wax. It's exciting. A janitorial dream—I mean, senior-head-of-custodial-support dream. And the best part? After school ends and everyone's gone for the summer, I get to pull out the wax and do it all over again. I'm telling you . . . I'm living THE LIFE.

But other things get accomplished during the three days they're gone on the trip. When I'm waiting for the wax to harden, I organize all the

3

teachers' closets, place all the P.E. equipment in new containers—with labels of course—and, if there's still time, I rearrange the tables and chairs in the cafeteria, just for fun. When the kids return and find the lunchroom set up in groups of equilateral triangles, it blows them away!

And to be supportive of the kids—since some of them are camping out for the first time—I, too, camp out at the school. I set up a campsite outside next to the blacktop and cook all my food over a fire pit. It's my way of "giving back." Plus, it gives me a perfectly good reason to purchase an entire case of beans 'n' franks.

But just between you and me . . .

[looks left, then right]

I am a little worried about this trip. EVERYONE remembers what happened last year. I just hope these kids don't run into such bad luck.

Meanwhile, I'll be here, supporting them by having my own "camp-in."

[pulls out a pad of paper and jots something down]

I'm going to need more flannel.

Trevor Jones

About to enter
school, pacing
nervously

8:28 a.m.

Excited? Absolutely not. I've been dreading this trip since the beginning of the year. It's not mandatory, but EVERYONE goes. Tradition, they say.

I heard there was only one kid in the history of Westside who didn't go on the trip, and that was Bobby Benson from three years ago. He was fortunate enough to have broken his ankle in a Vicious Volleyball Incident, and his parents wouldn't let him go.

That tells me there IS an excuse that will get me out of this ridiculous trip. Hopefully I won't have to break anything bone-like.

But did you hear the details? It's two nights away. TWO.

At a camp. In the woods. With bugs. And eighth graders.

Who in their right mind would be excited about that?!

Not me. That's why I'm not going.

Plus, I have an allergy to bugs that fly. Or walk. Or breathe.

5

Well . . . it's not exactly an "allergy." It's more of an "emotional response." I tried to explain to Mom that it's a real THING—that just the sight of a bug makes me lose self-esteem. But she still won't write a note to excuse me. All she did was narrow her eyes and say stuff about me expanding my horizons and enjoying my life and other crazy stuff like that.

But somehow . . . some way . . . I will find an excuse to get me out of this mess.

Maybe . . . oh!

[eyes light up]

I've got it! Our school counselor, Miss Plimp. SHE could write me an excuse! I'll simply explain to her that going on an overnight trip where eighth graders are present would do damage to my stress levels as well as my ability to form sentences. Corey Long has been pretty decent to me lately, but who knows if THAT will last? When it comes to acts of humiliation, the guy is hard to figure out.

Plus, there's a rumor going around that he's going to pull some pranks just like his brother did last year. So in my opinion, putting me in the vicinity of Corey and a campfire and his foot is just poor decision making.

I'm sure the school board wouldn't want any bad press. Not like the kind they got from the trip last year.

So I've made my decision. I'm staying behind.

Hopefully I can buff the floors with Wilson. There's a rumor that he also waxes the floors while everyone is away on the trip.

IT'S LIKE THAT RUMOR WAS MADE FOR ME.

6

Corey Long

Not all that
worried

8:29 a.m.

That incident from last year? It was my older
brother, Trent. He tried to pull a prank on his
cabinmates by hiding their deodorant in the bear-
proof box. But Trent is one of those dudes who
isn't big on things like DETAILS. He forgot to
lock the box. A bear got in there and ate all
the deodorant, along with a bunch of peanut but-
ter crackers. But I guess the crackers made the
deodorant taste good, and the bear caught the
scent of Trent's deodorant back in the cabin. Long
story short, when they got back from the campfire,
a bear had gotten into their cabin and ripped
open their backpacks and tore apart their sleeping bags.

It. Was. Awesome.

So anyway, there's this rumor going around that
I'm planning some pranks for this year's trip. It
happens to be true—I mean . . . I'M the one who
started the rumor.

Yeah, I've already picked out my prank victim. It was an obvious choice. I've just been so successful at humiliating Trevor this year, and these pranks are GUARANTEED to work on him. I hope the guy doesn't take it personally or anything—it's just business. It's my duty to uphold the reputation of the Long brothers. Duty calls, bro.

But there is one downside. My brother got in trouble with the principal last year. And the principal got in trouble with the park ranger. And next thing you know, the local newspaper had written an article about it. But here's the worst part: because of my bro's deodorant incident, we can't bring ANYTHING that has a scent. That means I can't bring my hair gel.

HOW WILL I SURVIVE, MAN?!

[shakes head]

I don't know. I just . . . don't know.

CHAPTER ONE

WESTSIDE MIDDLE SCHOOL BUZZED WITH EXCITEMENT. It was the last week of school, which meant it was time for the annual end-of-the-year overnight trip to Camp Whispering Pines. It was a longstanding tradition at Westside for all the students to attend, and everyone was looking forward to it, particularly the teachers, who would be given time off to finish report cards while Counselor Plimp and Vice Principal Decker supervised the students.

Since it was his first year overseeing the trip, Vice Principal Decker was busy in his office reviewing his overwhelming list of things to do. "Do I have all the emergency contact forms? Where is the emergency first aid kit? And where is my clipboard? I need a clipboard!"

He said all this to the wall.

Meanwhile, as Decker frantically prepared, the students of Westside were having energetic conversations about what to pack and which cabin they might be assigned. There were whispers about campfires and marshmallows. And elated squeals about being without parents for two nights.

To be fair, most of the squeals came from Cindy Applegate since this trip was going to be "the most awesomest thing ever!" in her words. She had tacked up a diagram of her packing plans on the outside of her locker. She bounced with enthusiasm as she shared it with her friends who'd gathered around.

Libby Gardner, seventh grade class president and world's biggest fan of label makers, pushed up on her tiptoes to get a good look at Cindy's drawing. Libby's list of items was much different, but after reading Cindy's, she decided to reword one of her own items. Everyone could benefit from a "totally cute toothbrush" (and a backup).

But one thing on Cindy's list caught Libby's attention, and not in a good way.

Watermelon-flavored toothpaste.

Had Cindy not read the gentle-yet-assertive letter Miss Plimp had sent home?

CINDY'S PACKING PLAN!

1. Daisy Pillowcase
2. Rainbow-striped sheets
3. Faux-fur comforter
4. Lime-green fuzzy slippers
5. Watermelon-flavored toothpaste
6. Totally cute toothbrush
7. Backup totally cute toothbrush
8. Precious stuff to decorate with!

Dear Families,

　　Your son or daughter is about to spend three glorious days at Camp Whispering Pines. It's a friendly and beautiful place where nature is in abundance and the wildlife will awe you.

　　While we will be spending our days learning about wildlife, we honestly don't want to learn TOO much about wildlife. Yes, I am referring to the Camp Whispering Pines Incident of Last Year.

　　So in order to keep bears and other predators out of the cabins, we will be adopting a No Scent Policy. This means items that smell fruity or sweet or musky or bubble gummy WILL NOT BE PERMITTED*.

　　(I apologize for the all caps, but I felt it necessary.)

　　Do not worry, as the school will provide all food as well as generic, scent free personal care items. Let's enjoy nature the natural way! Your child will thank me for not allowing them to become part of an investigative news article.

Sincerely,

Miss Plimp

Miss Plimp

*Note: Other items not permitted . . . food, candy, electronic games, cell phones, jewelry, high-heeled shoes, LEGOs, My Little Pony, regular ponies, and any clothing with a picture of a dog (but cat photos are perfectly fine!).

Libby pushed through the crowd and managed to make her way up to Cindy. "Didn't you read the letter Miss Plimp sent home?" Libby held up the letter for her, just in case.

"Yep, I read it." Cindy happily tossed her curled hair over her shoulder. Then she leaned in closer and spoke softly, hoping no one else could hear her. "Surely she didn't mean I couldn't bring my own personal toothpaste—I have to order it online because that flavor is not available in stores. It's superspecial."

Libby folded her arms. "No flavored *anything*."

Cindy clutched her stomach. "But whenever I change my routine, I get stress stomachaches."

Libby could understand this. She, too, suffered from stress stomachaches. But they usually came on when items weren't organized by color. She patted Cindy on the shoulder. "You will survive."

Cindy smacked her gum. "We'll see." Then she spun around to face her group of friends, who were still adoring her packing plan.

Libby hurried down the hall to class without stopping to talk to anyone else. Socializing about the trip was not something she was ready to do yet, since departure time was in less than twenty-four hours. There was still so much that had to be done.

Keeping in tradition with the trip, the students were allowed to have two social events at Whispering Pines. The first night was always planned by the eighth grade class president, and the second night was planned by the seventh grade class president. This meant the first social would be put on by none other than Savannah "Great Boots" Maxwell. And, of course, the second night was to be planned by Libby "Sensible Shoes" Gardner.

The problem was, for the first time in a long time, Libby hadn't come up with a detailed plan. She was paralyzed with fear. Savannah Maxwell wasn't just the owner of fabulous boots; she was Libby's mentor-turned-nemesis. She didn't respect Savannah's attitude, but Savannah was still considered the best class president in Westside history—a title Libby desperately wanted to hold someday. The thought of planning an event *after* Savannah's was just too much pressure. How could she ever top *the* Savannah Maxwell?

Libby had come up with a few ideas, but after looking over them, she was certain she was so doomed.

She had to make some party-planning decisions and quick! Whenever she desperately needed help, she knew exactly who to ask . . . her best friend.

Trevor Jones.

Just before the late bell rang in homeroom, Libby rushed

I am so doomed.

Ideas for the Social:
1. Pictionary
2. Arts & Crafts
3. A meaningful conversation corner
4. Literary Limbo!

HOLA!
Kitty Cat!

up to him and tapped his shoulder. "Help a girl out?"

"With?" Trevor turned around in his chair and smiled at her. When Libby asked for his help, it meant she was in full event-planning mode. It was her favorite mode, and any mode that was a favorite of hers was a favorite of his.

"The Wednesday-night social. I need big plans. BIG," she said. "But right now all I have is a list of things that need to be crossed out. It's not good."

Trevor took a deep breath, realizing that he hadn't told Libby yet about his plans to get an excuse to skip the trip. He sank lower into his seat. "Yeah . . . no."

"Does *yeah/no* mean *no*?"

He cringed. "Yeah . . . it means no."

"You won't help me?" Libby suddenly became concerned. This wasn't like him—helping her out was one of his favorite activities. It was right up there with eating Raspberry Zingers. Or pretty close.

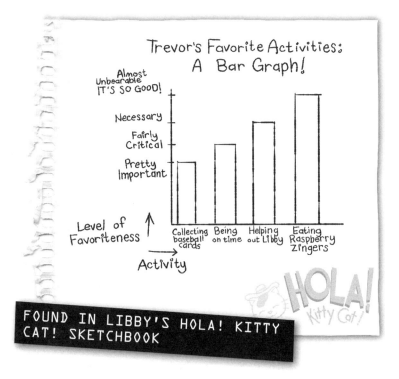

FOUND IN LIBBY'S HOLA! KITTY CAT! SKETCHBOOK

Libby squatted down next to him and whispered, "What's going on, Trev?"

He took a deep breath, and then the truth oozed out slowly, like Play-Doh. "I'm planning to . . . you know . . . find a way . . . to get out . . . of . . . like . . ."

She poked him. "Spit it out, Mr. Jones."

Trevor remembered that they used to play Sherlock Holmes when they were younger, and Libby always made the best detective. Trevor was good at being interrogated. And right now, Libby's tactics of interrogating were already beginning to work. "I'm trying to get out of going on the trip. It's not really my kind of thing, Lib."

"I don't think you have much of a choice. By *all-school*, I think they mean everyone. Including you, Trev."

But Trevor had been trying for months to *not* be included in this trip. He'd thrown out excuse after excuse to his mother—allergies, phobias, scheduling conflicts, possible meteor crashes—all in the hopes of getting out of it. In fact, he'd even studied survival techniques just to prove to his mother that he wasn't prepared for this trip.

With so many excuses, he had to keep track of them in his Wilderness Excuse Journal. Keeping track of them like this was perhaps overkill, but Trevor was determined to find an excuse.

Libby knew it was time to bring some reality back to Trevor's whirling brain. "You are going on this trip. You HAVE to."

"But it's a voluntary trip!" he yelped. "That means I don't *have* to go, according to the dictionary."

"It's tradition," she said.

Trevor narrowed his eyes at her. "Are you aware that black bears have nonretractable claws, which give them excellent tree-climbing ability? So even climbing a tree will result in my death-by-bear."

She sighed. "Trevor . . ."

"And did you know that mosquitoes can smell the carbon dioxide in your breath from over one hundred feet away?"

"Trevor."

FOUND IN TREVOR'S WILDERNESS EXCUSE JOURNAL

Wilderness
Excuse
Journal

Allergies:
• pollen
• paths made of dirt
• people who enjoy the outdoors

reaction

Phobias:
• bugs (all bugs)
• dining halls with some sort of "campy" food
• trees with leaves and/or bark and/or holes for woodpeckers
• going to the bathroom outside

Survival Skills Needed:
• If without water in the woods, add nine drops of iodine to stream water (I have a fear of iodine and of spelling the word iodine).
• If lost in the woods, use a yellow shirt or bandana to flag down rescuers (I own nothing yellow—it is just the worst).
• If crossing a deep river use water hyacinth and dried vegetation wrapped in a plastic bag as a flotation device (Any trip where a "flotation device" may be needed is a trip I DO NOT NEED TO TAKE, THANK YOU).

"And I bet you don't even know that mice can squeeze through incredibly small spaces because of their soft skulls, so any hole in the cabin means total infestation."

"Trevor! How do you know all this ridiculous information?"

"Research. I put a lot of work into finding a loophole for an excuse not to go. My mom wasn't fazed by any of these, either."

Libby patted him on the shoulder. "You'll probably have the best time of your life."

"Me? In the woods? Libby, the closest I've ever gotten to camping was when my mom got a flat tire and we had to eat snacks in the lobby of Tires Plus."

She smirked. "That was so brave of you."

"Exactly my point. I'm *not* brave. There's no way I can figure out what to do if there's a sudden bear attack. Or a need to replace a battery in a flashlight. Or if I can't find a microwave to heat up my evening hot chocolate."

She shook her head. He wasn't making sense. There had been so many things that happened this year that showed her he *was* brave. He'd handled eighth graders, mashed potatoes on the floor, speeches in front of the whole school, and evil Hollywood producers.

That was a lot of bravery. Why couldn't he see that?

Libby stood and planted her hands on her hips, super-hero style. "Trevor Jones, you'd be surprised to see how much you can handle when you're in a difficult situation. This trip will expand your horizons."

He squinted as he looked up at her. "Is that you, Mom?"

"I'm serious. Don't you think you've done a lot of stuff this year you never thought you would?"

He took a deep breath. It was true that he'd managed to put Corey Long in his place several times. He'd overcome his fear of speaking in front of people to help Libby win class president. And he'd managed to help run a famous designer out of town. So, yeah, maybe Libby had a point. But he never thought he'd have to apply any of these skills to the *outdoors*. "I can't do it, Libby. I'd rather focus on avoiding all difficult situations. That's probably a better use of my time."

Libby shrugged. "I hope you change your mind." She turned to head back to her desk.

"But I'll help you with planning the social," he called out after her.

"Thanks," she said as she sat down in her seat.

Trevor hoped he wasn't being unreasonable. He just figured he could learn a whole lot more about nature by writing a five-page report about it.

Wildlife

by Trevor Jones

FOUND IN TREVOR'S NOTEBOOK

Paragraphs.

Descriptive words.

Well-placed commas.

That's how he wanted to experience the outdoors.

And it was this argument that he planned to share with the school counselor, Miss Plimp. He pulled out the slip in his pocket to double-check what time he was supposed to meet with her. It read, *"Make sure you're not late, late, late! So our meeting can be great, great, great!"*

Trevor figured he should get there a little early since there would probably be a lot of students in line giving excuses for why they couldn't go on the trip.

Trevor didn't understand what type of person would actually LOOK FORWARD to sleeping in the woods with vicious woodland creatures all around. All with the possibility of not having nightly hot chocolate.

Who would want to do such a thing? Trevor wondered.

But then the answer hit him. There was *one* person who would be looking forward to every minute of this trip.

Marty Nelson.

Marty Nelson

Flipping through
the pages of
Extreme Ice Fishing

8:51 a.m.

ME. I'm pretty sure they have this trip every year
for me. In my honor, I guess. It's the one thing
I look forward to. This and Christmas, when I get
tons of new hiking gear as gifts. This past year
my mom got me a new Junior Survivor camouflage
vest. Hopefully it will help me get closer to
some wildlife. I've been collecting box tops from
my cereal so I can win a deck of vintage trading
cards with animal facts. But seeing animals up
close—IN PERSON—would be better than any card.
Though the badger card is pretty rare—a collec-
tor's item.

But hopefully I'll spot a raccoon or a skunk
or an opossum, or any other type of nocturnal
animal, really. Nocturnal animals rock. Since the
bathrooms are down the trail from our cabins and
I have "middle of the night" issues, I'll be sure
to spot a creature in the night.

[leans in closer, lowers voice]

But what I want to see most is a regular day-time animal . . . a deer. My plan is to spot a deer close to our cabin and then grab Cindy by the hand and say, "Look! A deer!"

Cindy thinks deer are supercute. This could be a big moment for me.

Yeah, I'm excited about this trip. Who WOULDN'T be excited?

Molly Decker

Hoodie pulled
tightly around
her head

8:52 a.m.

ME. I'm not excited about this trip ONE BIT. All that dirt and wildlife and . . . air. SO BORING. I mean, that's what Netflix is for. To watch this stuff in movies so we don't have to deal with it in person.

I'm sure there are other people out there like me—people who have no desire to go on an overnight camping trip.

We all have our reasons.

My dad once tried to take me camping. By the time he'd packed the bug spray, sunscreen, allergy medicine, Bactine, and poison oak repellent, he was exhausted and had to take a nap. When he woke up, it was too late to go.

In my opinion, anything that requires so much preparation that it brings on a nap should be illegal.

Like I said, watching movies is the only solution here.

25

Corey Long

Fidgeting with his hair

8:53 a.m.

My hair. That's the reason why I don't want to go. Vice Principal Decker sent home a list of items we can't bring, but it was mailed only to me. The guy went out of his way to make sure I didn't break the rules, simply because my brother did. But we're different people! So rude, man.

Oh, and at the top of that list? HAIR GEL.

It's like he wrote that just for me.

But without any gel, my hair is going to be . . . **[shakes his head and starts to walk off]**

So embarrassing. I can't talk about this anymore.

CHAPTER TWO

TREVOR KNOCKED SOFTLY ON THE OFFICE DOOR. "MISS Plimp? I have an appointment."

She was busy in the corner, carefully grouping her cat bobbleheads by color. "Orange tabby cats go here," she said under her breath, then looked up and noticed Trevor peeking in through the door. "Have a seat, dear. Be with you in a moment!" She turned back to her project. "Let's see . . . black-and-white tuxedo cats go here . . . all black go here . . . *aaaaand* done." She spun around to face Trevor, her hands clasped together as if something thrilling was about to happen.

For Miss Plimp, any time a student came to her for an appointment was an exciting moment. Too much of her day was spent organizing standardized tests, filing papers, and hunting down her missing coffee cup. Plus, there were all the cat decorations she had to manage—her job was exhausting!

But when a student needed to talk, she bubbled with excitement. She sat down across from Trevor and gave him her best enthusiastic smile. "You said you wanted to talk to me about the upcoming trip. You must be looking forward to—"

"I can't go."

"—fishing and hiking and trust exercises like—"

"I'm allergic to eighth graders."

"—falling backward into the arms of people you don't know and—"

"I'm also allergic to trust."

"—telling ghost stories around the campfire." She took a breath and tilted her head. "Did you just say you're allergic to trust? I don't believe that's in your permanent record." She started flipping through his file.

"It's not in there, Miss Plimp." He sat up on the edge of his seat. "I just have a feeling that putting me near anything that could turn into a humiliating situation is a bad idea. And stuff like campfires and rivers and bats and camp bathrooms just scream humiliation."

She smiled as if everything he'd just said was adorable—

like a three-year old with a lisp. "Aww, Trevor. You'll do just fine." She hopped up and patted him on the back as she motioned for him to leave. "There's a reason why we take you kids on this trip. There's a lot you'll gain from it—just trust the process."

"I'd rather trust the process of not leaving my house, thanks."

"I have so many great activities planned; there's nothing to worry about. I'll even come sit by you at *every single* meal."

He swallowed hard.

Oh, no. She's going to be my meal buddy?

Trevor decided right then and there that Miss Plimp was the wrong person to help him get out of this trip. After all these months of trying to get out of it, his final attempt was a bust.

"Want me to sign you up to lead our game of Trust Charades?" she asked. "The best way to deal with fear is to face it, you know. You could become a leader, Trevor!"

"No, no! I'm fine." He held his hands up and backed away slowly. "I can handle my fears. No need to put me in charge of anything. Thanks, Miss Plimp!" He turned and ran out of her office.

At the end of the hall, he stopped and leaned against a

wall to catch his breath. He had to go talk to someone else about this. The longer he talked to Miss Plimp, the closer he got to being put in charge of a game of Respect Limbo.

Down the hall, he noticed Vice Principal Decker heading into his office with his arms loaded with boxes of Band-Aids. This gave Trevor an idea.

He marched up to Vice Principal Decker's office door and knocked as he whisper-yelled through the crack in the door. "Can I speak with you, Vice Principal Decker?"

Mr. Decker opened the door slowly and looked Trevor up and down. "Are you trying to get out of the trip, too?"

Trevor nodded. "Yes, sir. Absolutely."

Decker opened the door and motioned to the only available chair—the rest were smothered with first aid items. "Have a seat."

Trevor sank into the chair and noticed the seat was still warm, obviously from the last student who had tried to get out of the trip. "Um, sir. I really need to stay behind. I have a fear of embarrassing situations."

Decker sat rigidly behind his desk and peered over a stack of permission slips. He shook his head. "Being embarrassed is not a good enough reason."

"Okay. I have an allergy to bugs." Trevor couldn't believe he had brought up this old excuse—a classic.

Decker narrowed his eyes. "Which bugs?"

Trevor crossed his legs and got comfortable. If he could think of a specific kind of bug, this just might work! "Bees, sir."

"We have first aid for that. What else?" Decker anxiously tapped his pen on his desk.

"You know, the kind that fly. And bite. And breathe air. Also, I'm even allergic to bugs that *don't breathe at all*." Trevor bit his lip as he thought through that one. He wasn't even sure if bugs *did* breathe air. Did they have little lungs? These were the kinds of questions that often popped up in Trevor's mind at inappropriate times.

FOUND IN TREVOR'S NOTEBOOK

Decker stood up. "Trevor, a fear of bugs—dead or alive—is not a good enough reason. Head back to class."

"But, sir. You said there was someone else who tried to get out of the trip. My seat was warm, so I know I wasn't the only one. How'd *they* get out of it?"

"Corey won't go without special permission to use hair gel, and Molly doesn't like oxygen. I said no to both of them. So pack your bags. You're going on this trip."

Trevor dropped his head and shuffled out of Decker's office. "Sorry to be a bother, sir."

Decker reached out and put his hand on his shoulder. "Give it a chance. You might just find this trip to be the best thing you've ever done."

"I seriously doubt it. But you're very good at optimism, sir."

As Trevor shuffled back to class, he thought about what Decker had said. Was it possible that he was right? That this trip would turn out to be one of the best things he'd ever done? He couldn't help but think of all of the humiliating situations he might face—hawks, caves, rivers, mud, dining halls, the need for bug spray—but then he imagined himself actually handling those situations without fear. Or worry. Or sweat stains.

Just as Trevor arrived at class, all that positive day-

Me, Captain Wonder Woods, dealing with stuff... LIKE A BOSS.

FOUND IN TREVOR'S NOTEBOOK

dreaming came to a halt. The intercom crackled, and Vice Principal Decker's voice boomed through the school.

"Students, I have an announcement. Our counselor has an important update for our upcoming overnight trip. Miss Plimp? Would you like to take the microphone and explain?"

In the background, Miss Plimp could be heard squealing with excitement. She grabbed the microphone and blurted, "Okay, Westside! We are going to try something new this year. I'm going to pair you up with a Sensitivity Buddy!" She squealed again and even clapped. "Your job throughout the trip is to compliment your buddy as much as possible. For example, Mr. Decker?"

A faint "yes" could be heard in the background.

"I like the way you organized the first aid kits."

He cleared his throat. "Really? Because it's still a jumbled mess, and I haven't had time to—"

There was the muffled sound of Miss Plimp cupping her hand over the microphone as she said to him, "Just say thank you and compliment me. We are modeling this for the students. On the *all-school intercom*."

"Yes, yes . . ." His voice sounded hurried and nervous. She uncovered the microphone, and Decker boldly stated, "You, Miss Plimp, have . . . great . . . handwriting."

There was a silent, awkward pause.

Miss Plimp then leaned into the microphone and continued. "I put a lot of thought into who will be partnered together, and I have no doubt it will be a positive experience. The pairings are now tacked up in the hallway, so stop by and check out who your buddy will be. No switching!"

The class groaned. Trevor bypassed the groaning and went directly to flopping his head on the desk. If his partner wasn't Libby or Molly, he knew this could easily turn into a disaster. But Miss Plimp *did* say she put a lot of thought into partnering people. Since Miss Plimp now knew all about his fear of trust, she'd surely pair him up with a good friend.

Surely.

"Now, let's make this the most complimentary trip yet, Westside!" Miss Plimp gave a happy clap, then turned off the intercom.

The bell rang, and Trevor fought the crowds to get a glimpse of the posters taped up in the hallway. He scanned for his name.

Trevor Jones, Trevor Jones . . . aha! He spotted his name. Then he traced the line with his finger, following it all the way across to find out who his buddy would be.

And he could do only one thing: his famous locker face-plant.

Trevor Jones

Hyperventilating
in the hallway

9:37 a.m.

Corey Long. He's my buddy. Can you believe his name and the word *buddy* are being used in such close proximity? Because I have no idea WHAT HE IS. Sometimes he acts like a friend, and sometimes he acts like I'm his prey—he's the hawk; I'm the mouse.

Hold on. I need to breathe deeply into this paper lunch bag.

[hyperventilates some more]

Whoa. I'm a little dizzy now. But all that breathing gave me an idea. I could fake a highly contagious disease. I'm sure I still have some leftover Halloween costume makeup. That's not weird.

Wait.

It totally is.

[goes back to hyperventilating in the bag]

I can't believe I'm going to have to give Corey compliments. What could I possibly say?

"You're doing a great job of tripping me on this hike!"

or

"Wow, you have successfully lowered my self-esteem!"

or

Oh, forget it. I have to find a way out of this trip, plain and simple.

A highly contagious disease may be my only hope.

Libby Gardner

Jotting down notes
on a clipboard

9:38 a.m.

I got Molly Decker for a partner. I think I'm okay
with this. Or maybe not.

[nervously taps pen on her clipboard]

See, Molly and I have been getting along quite
well lately. She helped me out during the school-
makeover debacle. She volunteered to get signa-
tures so we could get that rude interior designer
out of the school. AND Molly can totally keep up
with me when I power walk.

These are all good things.

But there is one thing about Molly that hasn't
changed: she's opinionated. Like . . . severely.

The girl lets you know EXACTLY what she's thinking. And sometimes her opinions hurt. One time she
called one of the school dances I planned "a total
snore."

Ouch.

And then there was the time she became my
campaign manager for student council president,

and she changed my slogan to "Vote for Libby, or Whatever."

Oh, and let's not forget all the times she pulled her hoodie over her head and pretended not to EXIST.

But then again, if I do have a very important decision to make on this trip—and I'm guessing I will—Molly is the perfect person to tell me her thoughts. Unfiltered, borderline hurtful advice might be EXACTLY what I need.

This could work!

Cindy Applegate

Simultaneously
bouncing and
grinning

9:39 a.m.

I heart this day so much! Even if Princess Kate walked in tomorrow to present me with the royal unicorn, TODAY WOULD STILL BE BETTER!

Miss Plimp paired me with Savannah Maxwell. Yep. Savannah More-Perfect-Than-the-Queen Maxwell. She's the eighth grade class president and has the BEST personality along with the BEST collection of knee-high boots. I will learn soooo much from her! I am about to make Savannah Maxwell my personal mentor!

Even if Princess Kate brought me a lifetime supply of Hubba Bubba Strawberry Watermelon gum, and even if that gum was in the trunk of a brand-new pink convertible, and even if that convertible had all the One Direction band members sitting in it . . . TODAY WOULD STILL BE A BETTER DAY!!

[leans in, looks left and right]

Now, don't tell anyone, but there's still one last issue to deal with before this trip. It's BIG, you guys.

Lucy. My kitty. She's just too cute to leave behind. We've never spent the night apart from each other, and I'm worried she'll have an emotional kitty-cat breakdown.

[gives a sneaky smile]

But don't worry . . . I have a plan.

Marty Nelson

Casually getting a
sip of water

9:40 a.m.

My partner?
[shrugs his shoulders]
Didn't even look.

Jordan Rossi

7th grader,
pretty pale

9:41 a.m.

M . . . M . . . Marty.

Marty Nelson is my—

[leans over, takes a deep breath]

He's my Sensitivity Buddy. That dude could squash me with his big toe. Maybe even his pinkie toe.

And I hear the guy is some sort of ninja survivalist. He probably won't even sleep in a regular cabin. He'll probably be suspended in the air on a rock face overlooking a waterfall.

But whatever. I'm not scared of him.

[bends over again]

Never mind. I'm scared of him.

CHAPTER THREE

TREVOR FELT THE HIGHLY-CONTAGIOUS-DISEASE EXCUSE might just work, but he wanted a second opinion.

At lunchtime, he spotted Molly in the far corner hunched over her lunch tray as she pushed corn around with her fork. He rushed over and slid into the seat across from her.

"Molly, I have to find a way to get out of the trip."

"I already tried every excuse to get out of it." Molly flicked her eyes up at him. "Trust me—he won't change his mind."

Then suddenly—for no clear reason at all—a smile started to form on Molly's face. It was super small, but with Molly any smile was a rare occurrence.

She scooched to the edge of her seat. "Look, we'll both

be there. And that's the only reason I'm . . ." Molly paused.

Trevor leaned in closer and narrowed his eyes. "The only reason you're . . . what?"

She bit her lip, hesitant about finishing her sentence. But she took a deep breath and let it out. "You're the only reason why I'm excited to go, okay?"

Even with all the bad fluorescent lighting, he could tell she wasn't just smiling. She was blushing.

"Sometimes it feels like you're my only real friend, Trevor," she said. "And if someone has to save me from a flying bat or gross food or a mutant frog, it'd be cool if it was you. Got it?!"

Trevor grinned. He liked that she got a little mean when she was being nice.

He stared at her for a moment. Molly sharing her feelings was all so new. He wasn't sure what to say. All that staring made him realize he liked the new electric blue highlights in her hair. But a hair compliment would probably be out of place at this moment. *What to say . . . what to say . . . ?*

Blink. Blink.

"Trevor, quit blinking at me. Whatever. Just forget what I said—"

"No, no! It's good. You sharing stuff is good."

Her face softened again as she looked at him, not saying a word. And suddenly, all his ideas about how he could get out of this trip disappeared. His fears, phobias, and allergies simply drained right out of him.

He had been worried this trip would turn into a disaster. That Corey Long would find a way to humiliate him in an epic way. That he would look like a loser in front of Molly.

But even if all those things did happen, maybe she *wouldn't* think he was a loser. She never had in the past. Without a doubt, Molly was a good friend to him.

It was time he was a good friend to her, too.

"I'm excited to go, too," he said. "You can protect me from humiliation, and I'll protect you from mutant frogs. Deal?"

She stuck out her hand and firmly shook his. "Deal."

Trevor Jones

Stunned by the
previous moment

12:05 p.m.

I can't believe that just happened. I just agreed
to go on this trip. We shook on it and everything,
so there's no turning back now. Maybe this trip
won't be a disaster. It is possible that Libby was
right—that I can handle more than I think I can.

So for now, I guess the best thing I can do is
pack for ALL emergencies.

For example: running out of water on a hike.
Or stepping on a rattlesnake. Or eating a burned
s'more. Or, heaven forbid, getting lost in the
woods with someone whose name rhymes with Borey.

[pulls out cell phone]

I need to call my mom. She's going to have to
get me a bigger bag.

Vice Principal Decker

Double-checking
his list

12:37 p.m.

I have checklists and checklists for my lists. I am ready. Even though I have a nagging feeling there is something I'm forgetting. That's probably normal, though.

It's quite important that this trip goes smoothly. Sure, I'll get complaints from parents about there not being enough gluten-free, dairy-free, fat-free meal options. The dining hall manager at Camp Whispering Pines is—how should I say this—quite rigid when it comes to requests.

So I have no doubt I'll get complaints about the food.

But I want this trip to go well because of my daughter. Molly is in her last week at Westside, and she's done an amazing job this year. She hasn't slammed her bedroom door as much, she hums happily when she touches up her highlights, and she's even made a friend. Maybe two.

I want her to end this year on a great note.

She needs to see she can make it through anything she faces. Even when things change, she will be fine.

I told her all that this morning on the ride in to school. But then I realized she had her headphones on the whole time.

[sighs deeply]

So I'm just going to do whatever it takes to make this trip great—

BATTERIES! That's what I didn't put on my list!

I'm going to rewrite my list and start all over again. Just to be safe. I don't want anything to go wrong.

CHAPTER FOUR

THAT AFTERNOON ON THE BUS RIDE HOME, LIBBY cheerfully bounced her knees. Trevor was sitting next to her and couldn't help but wonder what the joyous knee bouncing was all about. Plus, it was making him a little dizzy.

"Your knees are doing a happy dance becaaaaauuse . . ."

No answer—just a grin.

"You finished planning the Wednesday-night social?"

"Don't remind me. I'll get to that soon." Then she turned to face him, looking giddy. "This is about something completely different."

"Spill it."

"Okay, you know those survival TV shows where people are lost in the wilderness and have to figure out how to stay alive?"

"Please tell me that's not one of the activities you have planned for the social."

She ignored him and continued. "They always get back to the basics . . . no computers, no cell phones, no hair gel. And then you get to see what the people are *really* like. You see what kind of person they are without all those distractions."

"Is that a good thing?"

"Yes!" Libby clasped her hands together. "All this time Corey Long has been dropping hints that he likes me, but I could never be sure. Plus, he's been avoiding eye contact with me ever since admitting to liking me over the school intercom. Except I'm not sure I like him."

Trevor shrugged. "I'm no expert, but you liking him is probably an important part of both of you liking each other. See? That didn't even make sense."

Libby continued. "And so I came across this quiz in my *Pop Psychology* magazine called 'Is He Your Love, or Just Lame?' And there were a bunch of questions about likes and dislikes and what would he do if someone cut in line at lunch and got the last slice of pizza."

Trevor stroked his nonexistent beard. "Ahh . . . magazine quizzes—a reliable way to make all life decisions."

"It's a start. And now I'll get to see the real Corey on this trip . . . no hair gel. Just him—the *real* him. I need to see if Corey's my match." Her eyes lit up.

Whoa, Trevor thought. Libby's eyes are lighting up because of Corey Long?

He wasn't sure what to think of this. All her downright giddiness was because she planned to use this trip to determine whether or not she liked Corey. And not just *like* . . . but the gleam in her eye seemed to mean LIKE-LIKE.

Except Trevor had opinions about this. *Big* opinions. *OF COURSE COREY ISN'T A GOOD MATCH FOR YOU, LIBBY!* he considered shouting loudly. But then something she said changed his mind. "Did you say we're not allowed to bring hair gel?"

She nodded. "Cindy told me that Jamie told her that she overheard Brian tell Brad that they accidentally eavesdropped on Miss Plimp, who said Decker mailed a letter to Corey making sure he didn't bring hair gel. They're worried he'll turn out like his brother. We'll see, I guess."

Trevor formed a picture in his head of Corey hanging out around the campsite with absolutely no hair gel.

Trevor thought all this was perfect. Corey would show his true colors, and Libby would realize he wasn't good enough for her. And Trevor wouldn't even have to make some big dramatic scene explaining all this to her!

"It's a good idea, Lib. This trip and that magazine quiz

FOUND IN TREVOR'S NOTEBOOK

will probably tell you everything you need to know about that guy."

She smiled. "Right? It's the perfect time to see what he's *really* like." She leaned her head against the window and said softly, "I hope it works out."

As mailboxes and trees passed by the window, Libby imagined what it would be like witnessing Corey's *real* side. She worried that it was the hair gel that made him cool . . . confident . . . handsome . . . *dateable.*

Which meant she might see the worst side of him, even if he was all sorts of handsome at the same time.

Libby realized that Trevor was asking her questions about going on the trip, but he hadn't said one thing about wanting to get *out* of the trip. Had he changed his mind? She whirled around to face him. "So . . . are you going on the trip?"

He nodded as he stared down at his hands.

"That's great!" She elbowed him. "So Decker wouldn't let you use an allergy excuse, huh?"

"I changed my mind. I *want* to go."

Libby's eyes grew as big as truck tires. "You, Trevor Jones. *Want* to go?!"

Trevor didn't want to tell her he'd decided to go because of Molly. He had a strange feeling in the pit of his stomach—one he couldn't quite describe. He just knew he was excited Molly wanted him to go. Maybe this strange feeling in his stomach meant he LIKED-LIKED her?

Or it could've just been a bad burrito.

Trevor rubbed his temple at the thought of whether to tell Libby all his confused thoughts about Molly that seemed to be affecting his stomach.

Seventh grade was only getting more complicated by the minute. He sort of missed the days of being a second grader, when his list of worries was simple.

Libby crunched down on an apple left over from her lunch. "Do you want help with packing tonight? I'm all done. You could borrow my spreadsheet to help you." She then whipped out the spreadsheet and shoved the paper into his hands.

Trevor took one glance at the paper and felt a little overwhelmed by the headings. There were times, he felt, when his dear friend Libby was amazingly prepared for life. And then there were times when she was a little *too* prepared—freakishly prepared. This was one of those times.

Libby's Super Practical Packing Spreadsheet!

Toiletries	Bedding	Survival	Extreme Survival	Emotional Needs	Impromptu Dance Numbers
toothbrush	lucky pillow	flashlight	playing cards to heal boredom	photo of Mom & Dad	confidence
morning face cleaner	lucky blanket	batteries		Journal	
evening face cleaner	sheets (lucky or not)	"How to Survive" pamphlet		tissues	
just-for-fun face cleaner				powdered ranch dressing	
Totally cute toothbrush (and backup)					

"Thanks, Lib. But I got this," Trevor said in his best convincing voice.

She tucked her spreadsheet into her backpack and grinned at him. "This trip is going to be life changing; I can feel it." She folded her hands in her lap and gazed out the window, letting out a happy sigh. "*So many* things are going to happen, Trev."

He looked up at the roof and said under his breath, "Let's hope not."

WESTSIDE
MIDDLE SCHOOL

THE NIGHT
BEFORE

Cindy Applegate

Outside her house,
nervously bouncing
from foot to foot

5:45 p.m.

Okay, so, packing? It took me four and a half hours to implement my detailed packing plan. And it was SO worth it! I have the cutest packed suitcase EVER. Even if a Princess Unicorn Rainbow Fairy packed her bags for the Bahamas, I'd STILL have a more stunning bag.

I can't wait to show it to Savannah Maxwell, my Sensitivity Buddy and FBFFLFR. Future Best Friend for Life for Reals!

I am about to rock Savannah's boots off!

And I have one big surprise in store for everyone. You won't believe how much problem solving I used. Even Miss Problem Solver herself—Libby Gardner—will be impressed.

Oh my word, I am having the BEST DAY.

Molly Decker

Not really under-
standing what all
the fuss is about

5:55 p.m.

This packing thing is so easy. . . .
    Two shirts.
    Two skirts.
    One pair of boots.
    A toothbrush.
    And my stuffed Soul Bear.
    That's all I need.
    Now, let's get this over with. . . .

WESTSIDE
MIDDLE SCHOOL

DEPARTURE
DAY

CHAPTER FIVE

IT WAS SEVEN A.M. THE AIR WAS CRISP AND CHILLY. THE sun was rising.

Not a single person was excited about this.

Except, that is, for Marty, who was first in line. And there was also Miss Plimp, who happened to be a morning person. She was also an afternoon person. And an evening person. Overly Excited No Matter the Time of Day was her preferred state of being.

The mob of students huddled around the buses, all sleepy eyed and sluggish. The parent chaperones chugged from their coffee mugs in a desperate attempt to wake up. That's when Miss Plimp pulled out her megaphone and cheered, "Gooooood morning, Westside!"

The response was a collective "grrrrrr."

But she just smiled because she had so much good news to share. "I will break you into your Pal-Around Pods. Such a great name, right?" She didn't wait for a response (but technically she didn't get any). "This will be your group of eight that will share a cabin. And you'll all stay together for group hikes and Trust Walks!" Miss Plimp forged ahead down her path of positivity. "Now, let's give a round of applause to all our awesome chaperones!"

Trevor and a few students had woken up enough to clap for the row of parents standing at the back of the group.

Trevor popped up on his toes to get a better look at the parent volunteers. He recognized only one—Mr. Applegate, Cindy's father. Mr. Applegate didn't look up to acknowledge the clapping directed at him, because he was a rather busy man. Next to him was Cindy, looking very much like his daughter.

They were doing their signature "Applegate Power-Chew" since gum wasn't allowed on the trip.

Miss Plimp skipped around and grouped kids into their Pal-Around Pods. When she reached Trevor, she said, "You'll be with Corey, of course." She pointed over to Corey, who was yawning. "The rest of your group is already huddled behind him. They sure are eager!"

Or they're already trying to get on Corey's good side, Trevor thought.

"Can I ask you one question?" Trevor said just before Miss Plimp skipped off. "Why would you pair me with Corey? You know about our rocky past."

She wrinkled her nose and smiled. "I put a lot of thought into the partners. As I said before, trust the process."

"Trust the process," he repeated.

"Now you're getting it!" She patted him on the head and moved on.

Trevor had no idea what process she was referring to, and he certainly had no desire to trust it.

This is going to be a long trip.

As he got in line for the bus, he felt a hand on his shoulder.

"Have a great trip," Wilson said.

Trevor shrugged. "I'm not sure that's possible."

"As long as you're prepared, you'll do fine."

Trevor had brought along plenty of survival items, but he was suddenly clobbered with doubt. Had he brought everything he would need?

"What do I need to be prepared for?" The line moved forward. "And, um, could you tell me real quick because this line is really moving here?"

Wilson counted off on his fingers. "Carry water. Never eat a poisonous berry. If you're lost, stay where you are—rescuers will always find you. And never, ever touch a slimy doorknob. You don't need to know why . . . just trust me."

Trevor scratched his head. "Thanks?"

Wilson gave him a thumbs-up as he moved up in the line and onto the bus. Trevor's Pal-Around Pod was in the far back of the bus. He recognized only a few faces. The Baker twins—Brian and Brad (he still wasn't sure which was which).

And Corey Long.

(Of course.)

(Unfortunately.)

Corey stared out the window with his forehead pressed against it, not looking Trevor's way. There was an open seat right next to him. Except it wasn't just an open seat—it was the *only* open seat.

His heart sped up, doing double time.

I can't ride next to this guy for a two-hour bus ride! Trevor silently yelled.

He shut his eyes tight as he felt an overwhelming rush of panic wash over him. A panic tsunami.

But that's when a distinct smell filled the air. Strawberry watermelon.

"Excuse me, Trevor. I need to sit down." It was Mr. Applegate pushing his way through the crowded bus. He'd just finished power-chewing gum, and the smell still lingered.

"There's an open seat right here for you, sir." Trevor pointed to the open spot next to Corey.

"But where will you sit, son?"

"He can sit here!" It was Brian, or possibly Brad (no one knows, but who cares at this point!), pushing himself over to make room for Trevor. Luckily, the Baker twins were ultrathin, so there was plenty of room.

He plopped down in the seat and let out a sigh of relief. "Thanks, guys."

The seat was in front of Corey and Mr. Applegate. Trevor would have preferred his seat to be football fields away from Corey Long, but at least he wasn't sitting *next* to him. Trevor had no idea if Corey was going to be Nice Corey,

Halfway-Decent Corey, or Downright-Evil Corey, and that was so many Coreys to consider that Trevor wasn't quite ready to find out.

As the bus pulled away from the curb, Trevor leaned over to wave good-bye to the one person still left watching them leave.

Wilson.

He waved at the students and couldn't control the huge smile that filled his face. So much buffing and waxing was about to get done. These next few days will be the best, Wilson thought. Beans 'n' franks, here I come.

As the bus headed down the road, Brad-or-possibly-Brian Baker leaned over and said to Trevor, "I found out we're in Cabin Thirteen. Can you believe it?"

Trevor shrugged. "So?"

He felt a poke on his shoulder and turned to see Corey draped over the back of his seat. "Don't you know about Cabin Thirteen?" Corey's voice was low and far too menacing for Trevor's taste.

Trevor shook his head slowly and wished he *did* know something about Cabin Thirteen other than the fact that it was probably next to Cabin Twelve.

A wicked grin filled Corey's face. "Dude, Cabin Thirteen . . . is haunted."

Trevor Jones

At a gas station
rest stop

9:31 a.m.

Did you see what happened back there? There was a wicked grin on Corey's face. I knew it . . . he's back to being Up-to-No-Good-Corey. There was something about the way he used the word *haunted*— it was like it was his best friend or something. What is he up to?

But I can tell you, I am tired of trying to figure that guy out.

My plan is to use my strongest survival skill: AVOIDANCE.

I, Trevor Jones, know how to run away from anything.

Wilson

Happily buttoning his newly purchased flannel jacket

10:30 a.m.

And so it begins. Three days of silence. Three days of no students dropping things on the floor. Three days of no students getting their lockers jammed. Three days of—you know, I could go on forever.

First up, I need to set up my tent on the blacktop. But no need to worry—it's not like I'm going to suffer or anything. I brought a generator. Tonight I plan to watch a kung fu movie marathon and cook up beef Wellington with spinach frittata.

[whispers to the camera]

Honestly, the beans 'n' franks and fire pit are just for show.

CHAPTER SIX

AS THE STUDENTS EXITED THE BUS, TREVOR RUSHED ahead of everyone. Let's just get the haunting over with, he thought.

Trevor looked up and stopped in his tracks as he took in the scenery. The dining hall was a rustic log cabin with a large wraparound porch complete with wood rocking chairs. Up the hill were rows and rows of quaint cabins, all surrounded by towering pine trees.

Trevor couldn't help but notice the camp was far less dirty and dangerous and covered in poisonous spiders than he'd imagined it would be. It was practically . . . nice.

"Breathe the air," Vice Principal Decker announced, which made Trevor pause.

Trevor didn't understand why he'd suggest this given

that breathing was an obvious necessity for living. He lugged his overstuffed bag to a spot in the grass and did just as instructed—breathed the air.

Wow, Trevor thought. This is AMAZING.

While still having all the qualities of typical inside-a-middle-school air, Camp Whispering Pines air had so much more. There was a freshness. A crispness. An airiness!

His lungs filled quickly, and he suddenly felt as though he could think more clearly. His worries of sharing a haunted cabin with Corey, being a Sensitivity Buddy to Corey, having to take a Trust Walk with Corey . . . they all slipped away.

He took in another delightful breath and tapped Molly on the shoulder. "Did you do it yet? Breathe?!"

"I always breathe. I have to."

"*This* air, I mean. It's different, right?" He couldn't hold back his energetic smile.

"Is something wrong with you?" She folded her arms. "All of a sudden you're happy, or whatever this is."

He took another deep breath. "I don't know . . . I just think I might not have an awful time. Maybe I should try to be more positive."

Molly looked suspicious. "Sounds like you breathed in *too* much air."

"Yes!" Libby yelped as she skipped up to them. "Your positive face is much more enjoyable to be around. Don't you think, Molly?"

"No. His miserable face is perfectly fine."

Trevor couldn't help but laugh. Even when Molly was trying to give a compliment, it came out as horribly offensive. It was one of his favorite qualities about her.

But he couldn't help but wish Molly wasn't always leaning to the side of being miserable. And so far on this trip, she seemed even more miserable than ever. Was something going on with her?

He remembered there had been times in the past when he'd caught a glimpse of Molly smiling. But the smiles were always slight, like she was holding something back.

And then he had an idea. Maybe he could help Molly. Being positive . . . looking on the bright side . . . keeping Molly from being miserable . . . it would help her *and* take his mind off Corey.

A project. *That's* what he needed.

"I have an idea," he proclaimed. "I, Trevor Jones, am going to get Molly Decker to smile at some point on this trip. It won't be a slight smile. It won't even be a halfway decent smile. I'm talking a big, huge whopper of a smile."

Libby squealed with excitement. "I love it, Trev! You

should get Molly to smile so big that it blinds us all with its brightness!"

"Maybe I'll even get her to say something nice about the air, too?"

Libby bounced on her toes. "Perfect!"

Molly narrowed her eyes. "You two do realize you're talking about me like I'm not here."

"You." Trevor poked Molly on the shoulder. "You are my project."

She flicked her eyes up at him. "A project? Me?"

"If I'm worrying about you and whether or not you're smiling, then maybe I'll stop worrying about all the humiliation I'm about to face."

"Love it!" Libby said, all singsongy, as she danced off to her cabin.

Molly turned to face him and stuck a hand on her hip. "It won't work. You can't *make* me smile. I'll just end up letting you down."

Trevor tossed his backpack over his shoulder. Before heading off to his haunted cabin, he turned and said, "Nope. I *will* make you smile, Molly Decker." He shot her a sneaky grin. "Brighter than the highlights in your hair."

Trevor Jones

Outside (allegedly)
haunted Cabin
Thirteen

11:15 a.m.

I have no idea if I'll ever get Molly to smile.
But if I've learned anything from Libby, it's
this: when in doubt, do a project.

Projects are Libby's answer for everything.
Loneliness. Boredom. Hunger. Partly cloudy skies.
Any type of weather, actually.

And Libby seems happy on an almost-regular
basis, minus all the times she's freaking out,
which isn't all that often, honestly. So she's
pretty much got it all figured out. I'm lucky to
have her as my best friend. She's like the big
sister I never had . . . a smart, loyal, always-
on-the-hunt-for-ranch-dressing big sister.

Yep, I'm lucky.

Now I'm off to see if the Molly Project will
take my mind off the fact that I'm staying in
haunted Cabin Thirteen.

I have to admit . . . after seeing that Camp
Whispering Pines is—dare I say—totally nice,

even down to the startling fresh air they truck in, I'm starting to think this might not be such a bad trip after all.

That's right—Trevor Jones is going to try hard to be positive. This day will go down in history.

If the president wants to make a national holiday out of it, that'd be cool by me. The whole country could stay home and think positive thoughts while eating Raspberry Zingers.

Molly Decker

Sitting on a tree stump

11:20 a.m.

Trevor's in for a big disappointment. There's no way he'll be able to get me to smile and be happy and all that stupid stuff.

It's not because I hate the outdoors and field trips and bad food and fresh air.

I'm not happy because of something else entirely. It's something Trevor isn't going to like one bit.

[looks away for a moment]

I just have to find the best time to tell him the news. Is there ever a good time to share bad news?

And no, these aren't tears. I happen to have allergies when I'm around nice scenery.

CHAPTER SEVEN

MISS PLIMP CALLED OUT AFTER THE CAMPERS, "ALL right, kids! Time to get unpacked and organized. When the bell rings, head down to the dining hall for lunch. Then we'll take our first group hike this afternoon!" She clapped for herself and headed off to her cabin—a super deluxe cabin with air-conditioning and Internet access. Necessary, she felt, because she would later need to look up "cats being funny" on YouTube since her mental health was important when supervising middle school campers.

She opened the itinerary she'd made for the trip and checked off everything she'd already accomplished for Tuesday.

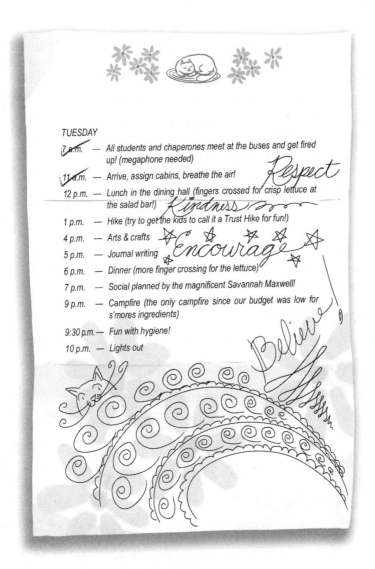

TUESDAY

7 a.m. — All students and chaperones meet at the buses and get fired up! (megaphone needed)

11 a.m. — Arrive, assign cabins, breathe the air!

12 p.m. — Lunch in the dining hall (fingers crossed for crisp lettuce at the salad bar!)

1 p.m. — Hike (try to get the kids to call it a Trust Hike for fun!)

4 p.m. — Arts & crafts

5 p.m. — Journal writing

6 p.m. — Dinner (more finger crossing for the lettuce)

7 p.m. — Social planned by the magnificent Savannah Maxwell!

9 p.m. — Campfire (the only campfire since our budget was low for s'mores ingredients)

9:30 p.m. — Fun with hygiene!

10 p.m. — Lights out

Respect

Kindness

Encourage

Believe

Trevor pulled open the door to Cabin Thirteen and cautiously stepped inside. There were four bunk beds, one in each corner of the room. The pillows looked fresh and fluffed. The blankets were warm looking and wrinkle-free.

If Trevor wasn't wrong, this cabin looked highly livable. And maybe even *not* haunted. But then again, it was only eleven thirty in the morning, and ghosts that haunt usually get their best work done after nine p.m.

Trevor was joined by the rest of his cabinmates.

The Baker twins.

Jake Jacobs.

Mr. Applegate.

A seventh grader everyone called Fishy, but no one knew why.

Where was Corey?

And they were short one camper. Who was going to sleep in the remaining bunk bed?

That's when he heard raised voices outside his cabin. He stepped out onto their front porch and saw Marty and Corey having a heated discussion while Miss Plimp listened and fanned herself with a Camp Whispering Pines brochure.

"I can't stay in Cabin Seventeen," Marty said. "There isn't a view of the woods, just the bathroom. I get freaked out if I can't sense when predators are lurking outside. There might be a serious bear problem here. Or general nocturnal-animal problem. There could be lots of problems."

Miss Plimp nodded and fanned. Nodded and fanned.

"I can't sleep on a top bunk," Corey said. "I have a fear of falling out and hurting my face."

Wow, Trevor thought. I had no idea Corey and I have the same fear.

Miss Plimp took a deep breath, then finally said, "Marty—you and Jordan switch to Cabin Thirteen since they have an extra bed. Corey, move to Cabin Seventeen and sleep on a bottom bunk. I don't want you to hurt your face."

Marty picked up his bag from the ground and marched toward the cabin. "No problem."

Whew! Luck IS on my side, Trevor thought. If Marty's with me, I might just survive this. Actually, with him around I can survive ANYTHING.

Marty stepped up onto the porch and approached Trevor with a determined look on his face. "Stop worrying. I'll take the bunk above you. We'll take shifts at night to patrol for bears."

Trevor shuddered. "B . . . b . . . bears?"

"Of course. This may be our only chance to see one in the wild and shoot it."

"Shoot?! Do NOT tell me you're going to shoot a bear!"

Marty smirked and reached into his bag. "Shoot it with this."

It was just a camera. *Whew.* Trevor took a deep breath to calm his nerves. "Shoot a bear with a camera . . . of course."

Marty laughed and slapped him on the back. "Why are you acting all nervous? You're not worried about this trip, are you?"

Trevor raised a brow. "Me? No. In fact, I'm busy with a project, actually. There's no time for worrying here."

Marty narrowed his eyes, not sure if he believed Trevor. *Cool and calm* wasn't exactly Trevor's middle name. "Whatever, bro. To survive this trip, you need to remember only one word: use your earplugs."

"Actually that's three—"

"The cabin chaperone is sleeping in here with us," Marty continued. "If my calculations are correct, Mr. Applegate is pushing forty-two, so there's a seventy-five percent chance of snoring. Plus, the earplugs keep you from hearing all the coyotes and—"

"Coyotes?!"

"—keep out the earwigs and the deadly Venchuga bug."

"The chuga WHAT?" His heart sped up. Even with all the Molly Project calmness he'd mustered up, the mere mention of a large bug was one of many things that immediately sent him to the "just-shy-of-about-to-pass-out" stage.

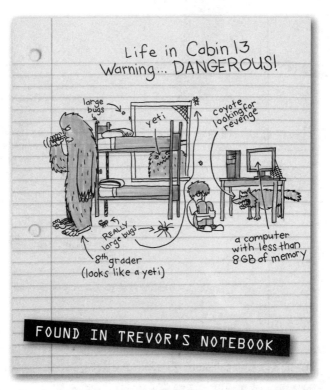

Life in Cabin 13
Warning... DANGEROUS!

large bugs

yeti

coyote looking for revenge

REALLY large bugs

8th grader (looks like a yeti)

a computer with less than 8 GB of memory

FOUND IN TREVOR'S NOTEBOOK

"Calm down. I'm a survivalist. Here—I brought an extra pair." Marty shoved the earplugs into Trevor's hand. "This is all you need."

Fortunately for Trevor, Marty was going to be sleeping right above him, so maybe all his sudden worrying was a tad much. And maybe—just maybe—Marty was right: earplugs were all he needed. Trevor's heart rate slowed. "Thanks, Marty. I'm calming down now."

"Good." He smirked and lifted a finger in the air. As if he were magic, the lunch bell rang. "Because we're about to enter the belly of the beast. The dining hall."

Marty Nelson

Cleaning the lens of his camera

11:39 a.m.

Nah, I didn't change cabins because of the view. I knew Trevor would be freaking out that Corey was in his cabin. And freaked-out people make bad decisions when they're deep in the woods.

So I had to make sure I was there to help him out. Just don't tell Trevor. I want him to think he can survive this all on his own.

I wish it were true.

Miss Plimp

Picking lint off
of her CATS ROCK!
sweatshirt

11:40 a.m.

Wow, this is all going swimmingly, right? The bus ride was nice. The weather is perfect. The kids are processing their feelings in a positive manner without resorting to name-calling or making faces. Though it's been only ten minutes. But still . . . I love it!

And all my plans are falling into place. The Pal-Around Pods. The Sensitivity Buddies. The Trust Walks. It's going to be fantastic!

I am just pleased as punch that Vice Principal Decker asked me to be in charge of the trip this year. It's the perfect setting for working on social skills goals. In my preplanning I even searched online—that means "Internet Google"—and found some fun ideas for field trips! Which means I have a few other things up my sleeve.

[leans in, winks]

Never underestimate a middle school counselor.

CHAPTER EIGHT

OVER IN CABIN FOUR, LIBBY, CINDY, MOLLY AND their cabinmates were rushing around unpacking their bags in a hurry so they could get down to the dining hall.

Correction: Molly wasn't actually rushing.

She was busy with a Sudden Boredom Nap.

Libby wasn't just unpacking; she was organizing her space. She set down her last item and stepped back, proudly admiring her work. "Perfect!"

Molly grunted, then sat up. "Finally. I've been unpacked for half an hour."

Libby glanced at Molly's shelf underneath hers and realized why it hadn't taken Molly nearly as much time.

Libby looked over at Cindy, who wasn't organizing her space . . . she was *decorating* her space. "Cindy, do you really need your bunk to be wrapped in ribbon?"

"If it's not just like home, I get nightmares."

"You have glitter hearts taped to your bed frame at home?" Cindy tilted her head. "Who doesn't?"

Molly stood up. "Me, for one. All this glitter is making me nauseous. Take it down, Cindy."

Libby stepped into the middle of the room and held her hands out—referee style. "Everyone's entitled to have their space set up how they'd like it. Even though this IS a camping trip and I'm not sure why you'd need all the boy band posters, Cindy."

"I want to impress my Sensitivity Buddy," Cindy said. "Don't you think Savannah will love it? The girl has serious style."

Libby sighed. She'd been down this road before—the

road of trying to get the approval of Savannah Maxwell. But it was a dead end. Libby had learned the hard way that, even though Savannah was eighth grade class president and severely stylish, she wasn't a particularly nice person. "Be careful," Libby warned as she narrowed her eyes. "Her niceness can turn to meanness just like THAT." She snapped her fingers.

Cindy stepped back. "Did you just go Full Mobster Wife on me?"

Molly said under her breath, "Whoa, that was awesome."

"Sorry." Libby blushed. "I guess I get a little overprotective of my cabinmates."

"Well, thanks for looking out for me," Cindy said. "But I got this."

Their chaperone, Mrs. Steiner, poked her head into the cabin. "Let's all settle down and head to the dining hall." Mrs. Steiner gathered a few girls and started for the door. "Meet us there!" she called out behind her.

Just as they left, another girl marched inside the cabin.

"I'm here!" Savannah charged into the middle of the room like she was leading a marching band. Before she could even set her bag down, she looked over at Cindy's bed and gasped.

"Oh. My. Cuteness!" She pointed over at Cindy. "HOW-DIDYOUDOTHISANDWHOAREYOU?!" she blurt-yelled.

"Me?" Cindy hugged herself and blushed. "Where do I start? First, I'm Cindy, your Sensitivity Buddy. We met in the parking lot. And you sat next to me on the bus. Um . . . let's see. . . ."

Savannah threw her bag on the bottom bunk. "Tell me everything about your decorations."

"Well, I made most of them myself, cutting pictures from magazines and making an inspiration board, then—"

Savannah held her hand up. "All I want to know is if you can do the same thing for *my* bed."

"Decorate yours the same as mine? Like twinsies?" Cindy bounced on her toes. "Of course!!!"

"Awesome." Savannah twirled around and headed for the door. "And make sure you unpack all my clothes—no wrinkles!"

"Absolutely!" Cindy called after her.

Both Libby and Molly crossed their arms and glared at Cindy.

"Be careful," Libby said. "That girl will use people for whatever she can get."

Cindy waved her off. "She's not using me; she's asking for my *expertise*—there's a difference."

"Fine." Libby grabbed her backpack. "The bell rang—we should all get down to the dining hall." She glanced at Cindy. "Are you coming?"

She started rummaging through her supplies. "Y'all go ahead. I have to turn Savannah's bunk bed into Bunk Bed–Tastic! Toodles!"

Molly turned and bolted out the door. Cindy's vocabulary made her ears hurt.

Libby trailed behind Molly and whispered over her shoulder, "The purple fur comforter is totally over-the-top."

"It's *all* over-the-top," Molly said.

All alone in the cabin, Cindy pulled out her remaining precious decorating items and set them down on the floor.

But then a strange thing happened.

Her bag moved.

It moved again.

Something was in there!

Through the opening of her bag, a head appeared. A furry black head with two white stripes.

There was a skunk in Cabin Four.

Cindy Applegate

Giggling

11:42 a.m.

No, no, no. Hold up, everyone—settle down.

It is NOT a skunk.

It's Lucy, my painfully adorable cat. Remember how I mentioned my kitty and I can't be apart and that I had a plan? Well, THIS is my plan!!

Last night I put temporary white hair dye on her, two stripes down the back, and VOILÀ! Lucy has been skunk-i-fied.

Now she can just hang out near our cabin and everyone will think she's a regular woodland creature and leave her alone. My dad won't even be able to recognize her.

At night after dinner, I can sneak her into my bed to snuggle. It's the perfect plan!

Except.

Hold on. . . .

[digs through her suitcase]

Oh, no. Dinner. I didn't bring her any food! What am I going to do?!

[paces nervously around the cabin]

I also don't have a litter box! Or any adorable holiday sweaters!!! THIS IS A DISASTER.

Unless you feed Lucy from a package that has the word *fancy* on it, she will DIE. And if she doesn't have a change of sweaters, she'll lose all her dignity.

And if my father finds out that I snuck her here . . . he will ground me for years. I won't be able to go to the mall until I'm the legal voting age.

I need help. FAST!

And as weird as it sounds . . . there is only one person here who would know what to do in an animal emergency.

Marty.

CHAPTER NINE

THE WALLS OF THE DINING HALL WERE MADE OF RUSTIC wood. The ceilings were made of wood, too. And the floors. And the tables.

It was all-around very woody.

Metal chairs were neatly placed next to long tables covered in blue-and-white-checkered tablecloths. And the giant room smelled like pinecones and spaghetti.

What's so bad about this? Trevor wondered.

And then it happened. The cafeteria manager stormed out from his office and bellowed, "SIT. DOWN." The man towering over all the students was large, unshaven, and smothered in flannel. He was one ax shy of being a folktale character. "I am Mr. Skeely, and you will listen to EVERY WORD I SAY."

The students scrambled to chairs, and the room quickly

became silent. Trevor was relieved that in his mad dash to sit down, he'd ended up next to Marty.

There was a calmness in Marty's eyes, a kind of confidence that Trevor hadn't seen before. It was as if Marty was in his element—the woods, the fresh outdoors, the predatory animals somewhere nearby—and it brought out his inner self. That, or he ate a really good breakfast.

Marty patted Trevor on the back and whispered, "Like I said—we're in the belly of the beast. Do whatever this man tells you. If you get him on your side, this trip will be smooth sailing. Trust me."

Trevor nodded in agreement because whenever Marty ended advice with "trust me," it meant he should do just that. He turned to pay attention to Mr. Skeely, who was busy rifling through a stack of posters, hunting for something. "Aha. Found it."

Mr. Skeely lifted up a poster that had words and straight arrows and squiggly arrows and arrows that didn't seem to serve a purpose and arrows that weren't even arrows. "Just read this poster, and it will all be clear." Mr. Skeely had lowered his voice so all the students had to lean in to hear his every word. "We have a system in this cafeteria, and you are not to break the system. There were some problems last year, so I updated the flow. To get your food, line up here." He pointed to objects on his poster as he explained. "For cold plates, go here; hot plates, go here; milk products are here; juices here; forks on this side and knives on the other. Do it all IN ORDER. Just follow the new and improved flow—it's easy."

Trevor squinted to get a better look at the poster, but the more he looked, the more he became seasick.

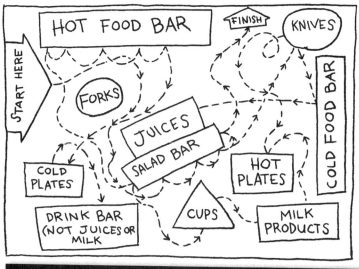

SKEELY'S NEW AND IMPROVED FLOWCHART

"And for cleanup, all things flow counterclockwise, and the chairs are to be stacked five high and placed in the southwest corner during winter and northeast in spring. There's a flow, and you are not to mess up the flow. Just remember: FLOW. Got it?"

Trevor didn't get it. No one seemed to get it.

"Got it!"

Except for Marty.

Mr. Skeely squinted to get a better look at Marty, then pointed directly at him. "YOU. I remember you from last year. On the first day you picked up your fork first and messed up the flow."

Marty stood and spoke in a way Trevor had never heard before. "Yes, sir. But I learned from my mistake, and I became an example for the others who made the mistake of getting a fork first. And if it happens again, sir, I can help out this year. Sir."

Mr. Skeely tugged on his beard as he thought this over. Finally he grumbled, "Okay, kid. You can help with flow management."

Then Mr. Skeely stood up straight, and Trevor was sure he had just added a good six inches to his height, probably out of sheer willpower. Skeely was quite impressive, if one was impressed by highly flanneled almost-giants. By the look on Marty's face, Trevor could tell he was *highly* impressed.

"For lunch we have spaghetti or salad. Except we're out of lettuce right now."

There was a gasp from the back of the group. Miss Plimp

clenched her jaw and quietly coached herself. "No salad. I . . . will . . . stay . . . positive."

Skeely pointed to the poster and said, "Go ahead and line up to eat."

But no one moved. The entire cafeteria froze. There was no way someone was going to attempt the directions on that poster and mess up the new and improved flow—it looked impossible.

It was Marty who stood first. He knew exactly where to go, and as he approached the food line, the entire school quietly folded in and lined up behind him, following his every move.

Marty beamed as he led the line, determined to impress Skeely with his leadership skills.

Just as Marty reached for his plate, he noticed something out of the corner of his eye. Someone had rushed through the cafeteria doors. Late.

That latecomer rushed past everyone and marched right up to Marty, hands on hips.

So upset that even the curls in her hair were flustered, Cindy whispered in a shaky voice, "Th . . . there's a cat . . . in my room."

"What kind? Bobcat?"

"No."

"Panther?!"

"No."

"A lion. You saw a lion!"

Cindy threw her hands in the air. "Lucy—my house cat! SHE STOWED AWAY!"

"Keep your voice down." Marty glanced over at Skeely to make sure they weren't being watched. Luckily he was busy whittling a stick. "Stowaways are in boats," Marty explained. "There's no boat here."

"She was in my bag. My big fancy bag!" Cindy leaned in closer to make sure no one heard what she was going to tell him next. "Listen, when I say *stowed away*, what I mean is I disguised her as a skunk and packed her up myself."

Marty stood motionless and stared at her, stunned by this piece of news.

"Stop staring at me! I HAD to do it—she is fiercely adorable, and we can't be apart. But admitting I painted my cat to look like a skunk sounds like I'm a crazy person, so you need to feel super honored that I'm admitting this to you. Can I get your help or what?"

Marty stuffed his hands in his pockets. As much as he didn't want to have anything to do with a domestic cat, he couldn't help but be honored that Cindy would ask for his help. And also admit she'd done something super crazy. "What do you need?"

"Well . . . I didn't exactly think this plan through, and I have no food for her. Or cute sweaters. This means she could DIE. What do I do?"

To Marty, if there was one thing in this world that excited him, it was a wilderness emergency. It sounded as if this emergency was *made* for him.

Marty stood up nice and tall. "Meet me at your cabin just before the first hike. I'll fix this." He then poked her on the shoulder and smiled. "Now go get in line, and don't ruin the flow."

Cindy grinned from ear to ear. "I have no idea what that means, but I'll do whatever you tell me, Officer." She saluted him and skipped to the back of the line, grinning at the thought of tough Marty Nelson saving her adorable skunk-kitty.

Mr. Skeely

Dining hall manager
and possible giant

12:41 p.m.

Sure, I'll give that Marty kid a second chance. He seems like he might have some promise. It's possible that if he keeps up with proper cafeteria flow and switches over to flannel rather than camouflage, he'd be perfect for camp cafeteria management.

We'll see if Marty has the leadership skills.

I'm doubtful, though. But that's what dining hall managers do . . . doubt people.

CHAPTER TEN

"**S**HOW ME WHERE SHE IS." MARTY PACED THE FLOOR of Cabin Four.

"In my bag, like I said." Cindy fluffed her hair in the mirror she'd attached to her bed frame.

Marty peered into her bag—pink with purple polka dots—but saw only neatly folded shirts. "Nope. She's not in here."

"What?!" Cindy frantically scampered around the cabin. "Lucy? Lucy?! Where are you? Come out! Do you need a kitty massage? A kitty pedicure?"

Marty clamped down on her shoulder. "Stand still and think. If you were Lucy and disguised as a skunk, where's the first place you'd go?"

"The spa."

Marty rolled his eyes. "She's an animal. When she realized she wasn't at home, she probably got scared. And when animals get scared, they—"

"Go to the groomer."

"—seek protection." He sauntered over to her bunk bed. "My guess is she's hiding under here." He lifted the blanket without even looking under the bed. Within a couple of seconds, a furry head poked out.

Meow.

"Lucy!" Cindy plopped down on the floor and threw her arms out in anticipation for their giant reuniting hug. But scared little skunk-i-fied Lucy retreated farther back under the bed.

"Oh, no. This is so unlike her. She usually pounces on me and smothers me with cuteness. What should I do?" Cindy looked up at Marty with her best Help-Me-I-Need-a-Miracle face.

"Hand me one of the shirts in your bag," he said. "Right now, she needs shelter and to feel safe. I'll make a bed for her out of one of your shirts—that way it will have your scent on it to remind her of home."

"PERFECT!"

She began rifling through her bag, searching for the best shirt for the occasion. "Can't use this one, need it for hiking. Need this one for nighttime campfire. This one is perfect for brushing teeth. . . ."

"Anything! We don't have much time before Miss Plimp calls us down for our first hike. Just pick one."

"Aha! We can use this one. I brought it as a third backup in case we have an impromptu talent show."

Marty snatched it from her, folded it into a bed shape, and slid it under the bed for Lucy.

Throom! Lucy kicked the shirt back out to Marty.

Cindy's mouth dropped. "Why won't she take my shirt? That's the softest third backup shirt I have."

Marty scratched his head. "Maybe she likes the rustic outdoors?"

"No, no, no. Not MY kitty. She has no tolerance for anything rustic."

"Fine," Marty said. "Let's just find her some food."

Cindy winced. "Uh. That's sort of a problem."

"Don't tell me she won't eat unless she gets a pedicure first."

"Nah." She waved him off. "That's only on Wednesdays. The problem is she won't eat any food unless it's labeled with the word *fancy*. It's her signature quirk. I kind of like it, don't you?"

"Her quirk is making this impossible."

Cindy dropped her head, knowing this was a lost cause. "It's no use. We're at an outdoor camp, and the cafeteria manager is a Viking. There's *no way* he has any fancy food in that dining hall."

Marty took a deep breath as he considered whether he'd taken on a project too hard to solve. Fancy cats weren't exactly his specialty. But he wasn't the type to give up.

After all, he'd watched enough *Extreme Pet Makeover* to know there was always a way to turn your pet around. "Don't worry about it," he said confidently as he led Cindy out of the cabin. "I've got it all figured out."

Cindy Applegate

Feeling calmer,
sort of

12:55 p.m.

I am NOT going to panic. First of all, it's a dream come true to finally spend the night away from my house AND have Lucy with me. As long as she survives and keeps her dignity, it will work out. But I guess that's everyone's goal in life, not just my cat's. Was that too deep?

But this won't be easy. I am going to have to find a way to knit her a new sweater, because otherwise, all of that dignity? ALL. GONE. Lucy is a fierce dresser, and she won't stand for anything less than perfection.

I taught her everything I know. She's a good listener. Also? I can't believe I just admitted I talk to my cat about fashion. I'm really getting deep here!

Maybe y'all can edit that out?

Wouldn't want to sound flaky or anything.

Okay, gotta run! It's time for our first big hike, which means I'll finally get to hang out with Savannah Maxwell. I have SO many things I want to say to her. Then I'll probably leave time available for her to ask me questions. I'm sure she wants to hear all about my hair conditioner that gives my curls this bounce. And also about where to find great sales on glitter.

Big day ahead. BIG.

CHAPTER ELEVEN

"**S**TUDENTS, GATHER AROUND!" MISS PLIMP announced through a megaphone. She was taking the lead on directing the students because Vice Principal Decker—though he'd dressed in appropriate hiking gear—wasn't much of a hiker.

Truthfully, Miss Plimp was elated to be the one leading the group. This trip was the highlight of her year. "Time to partner up with your Sensitivity Buddy," she said with enormous enthusiasm.

All the students followed her peppy instructions and disassembled and then reassembled into pairs. Trevor could see Corey heading toward him, walking with his usual Superman-sized confidence. Even though Corey had changed cabins, he was still Trevor's Sensitivity Buddy.

Corey stepped up to Trevor and stood in *front* of him, not beside him, blocking his view. The Sensitivity Buddy walk was not getting off to a good start.

Keep focused on the Molly Project, Trevor told himself.

He glanced over at Molly, who was busy ripping the corners of her name tag. Trevor cleared his throat to get her attention. When she looked his way, he smiled and gave her a double thumbs-up.

But there was no response from Molly. No smile. Nothing.

So he attempted his Evil Villain face—high arched brow, menacing side-smirk—the one that always cracked up his mother.

Aaaaaand nothing.

Molly went right back to name-tag ripping.

Getting Molly to smile was going to be a bigger project than Trevor had expected. But this was good—it would keep him busy.

Miss Plimp divided up the groups and matched them with their camp counselors. Luckily, Trevor's group was paired with Libby and Molly's group. At least he'd have their support should everything go horribly wrong.

Not that Trevor thought that it would, given that he was now attempting to look on the bright side and all.

Miss Plimp walked/skipped up to Trevor's group and said, "I want to introduce you to your camp counselor and wilderness guide . . . Tad!"

This "Tad" was a man in his twenties who dressed like he was a cover model for *Outdoor Magazine*. He wore: a crisp, sporty shirt; expensive-looking hiking pants (multiple! pockets!); and even more expensive-looking hiking boots.

"Good afternoon, dudes and dudettes!" he said with a wink.

Molly was already rolling her eyes. This will be a long day, she thought.

"Looks like we have a group of about sixteen of you. I have plenty of snacks for you guys on today's hike."

The group—all sixteen—wiggled with excitement at the mention of the word *snacks*.

Tad dug around in his expensive-looking backpack, which wasn't worn at all. It looked as though he'd never even taken it on a hike. "I have raw almonds, prunes, and organic granola."

There was a collective deflating of excitement, like sixteen popped balloons.

"And I have trail maps for you," Tad said. "Keep them in your backpacks—no sense in getting lost in the wilderness!"

Trevor felt Tad's tone was a little too peppy for the phrase *getting lost in the wilderness*. And once Trevor got a look at the map, he realized that that phrase deserved its own scary theme song.

Trevor's hand shot up in the air. "Tad, can we take Paradise Trail?"

"Sorry, little dude. That trail is reserved for staff only. Today we tackle Bone Breaker Trail. But don't worry; it's totally safe as long as you don't fall and break anything."

The students stared at him in stunned silence.

Miss Plimp must've sensed their fear because she stepped right in and said, "Hey, I know! Now is the perfect time for you to give a compliment to your Sensitivity Buddy!"

There was an awkward pause among the students. And an even *more* awkward pause between Trevor and Corey. Then at the same exact moment, they both looked up and stared at each other. Their eyes then simultaneously drifted. Then they both flicked their eyes up and stared at each other. A pattern formed.

Stare. Drift. Stare. Drift.

The awkwardness continued over on the other side of the group, where Cindy had happily sat down next to Savannah.

Okay! Let the compliments begin! Cindy thought.

But that's not what happened.

"Did you get my bed decorated?" Savannah asked.

Cindy fidgeted with the cap on her water bottle. "Um,

see . . . there was an emergency. A wilderness emergency."

"Get it done. I want it cute," Savannah snapped.

"When we get back—I promise."

Miss Plimp approached the girls and gave a disapproving look. "Compliments, please."

Cindy pulled together some words and put them in a sentence.

"This is a nice log."

Savannah quietly responded, "I like your log compliment."

And then they both sat in silence.

Miss Plimp moved on and delivered the same disapproving look to Trevor and Corey, who also were sitting in silence, not giving compliments. With Miss Plimp looming over them, Trevor took a deep breath and finally let a compliment spill out. Sort of. "You have . . . shoes."

Miss Plimp clasped her hands together. "Add an adjective to make it a compliment."

As she floated on to give advice to other troubled pairs, Trevor took a moment and rethought his statement. What could he say about those shoes? They were the same ones that had tripped him repeatedly this year. They were the shoes he would have liked to never look at again. And now he had to compliment them?!

Surely I can come up with one word to describe his shoes. One word!

"You have . . . um . . ." Trevor stammered, ". . . *two* shoes."

Nailed it.

Corey glanced down at his feet. "Wow. You're right."

"Okay, your turn," Trevor said. Finally, Corey was going to have to say something, and it couldn't be a statement that was detention-worthy. He was starting to think this Sensitivity Buddy idea wasn't so bad after all.

Just as Corey opened his mouth, Tad threw his backpack over his shoulder and said, "Kids! Time to tackle this trail!"

Corey shrugged his shoulders. "Oh, well. No compliment for you." And he smirked at Trevor.

But it was an unusual smirk.

Trevor had memorized all of Corey's smirks, and this one was highly unusual. It wasn't the intimidation smirk. And it wasn't the "How do I tell Libby I like her?" smirk. And it wasn't even the "My mom picked me up in the station wagon, not the Range Rover" look.

This one was in its own league.

And Trevor Jones did not like smirks in their own league.

Not one bit.

Corey Long

Confidently leaning
against a tree

1:10 p.m.

That smirk? Yeah, it's a pretty unique one. Been working on that one for a while—it doesn't even have a name yet.

See, I'm not going to mess with Trevor on the hike. I have much bigger plans in store for tonight.

[leans in, gives a sneaky grin]

Since he's in Cabin Thirteen, I think it's my duty to see to it that Trevor thinks his cabin is haunted—VERY haunted.

When the sun goes down . . . he's in for a fright.

Gotta make my brother proud. In fact, those were his last words to me before I left: "Make me proud."

It's not often that my bro says stuff like that to me. It's not often he says ANYTHING to me. So I can't mess this up.

Especially since he also gave me some specific advice. "Vaseline on toilet seats is BOSS."

Not everyone has a brother that cool. I'm pretty lucky.

CHAPTER TWELVE

TREVOR DID HIS BEST TO STAY FAR AWAY FROM **COREY.** It wasn't all that hard, since Corey trailed right behind Tad as they hiked, asking questions about what time it gets dark and where he could find some clanging pans. But Tad was much more interested in pointing out things on the trail—small twigs, large twigs, and how clean his vest was!

Luckily Marty was hanging out at the back of the line, so Trevor stayed close to him. Marty wasn't very interested in the information Tad was giving out, and instead, he was busy picking berries. He gazed down at a dark berry in his hand. "Perfect. Nonpoisonous," he whispered.

Trevor peered over his shoulder. "Why are you collecting berries?"

Marty startled. "Why? Because . . ." He hesitated since he couldn't explain what he was *really* doing. "I, um . . . I collect berries and weedy grasses to study. At home. Under a microscope. It's normal, completely normal."

Trevor narrowed his eyes. For some reason, Marty seemed a little shifty.

"Oh, cricket!" Marty hurried off. He scooped up the bug and stuffed it inside his bag to add to his collection.

Trevor didn't understand. He wasn't a big outdoorsman, but he figured you were supposed to leave the outdoors . . . *outdoors*? Why was Marty putting All of Nature in a bag?

Then he noticed Marty had sneaked off to talk to Cindy. He showed her the bag but shielded it, trying to make sure no one else saw. But Trevor did.

Then it all made sense to Trevor. The bug, the girl, the shifty behavior . . . Marty was trying to impress Cindy by showing her "icky stuff." It was a little third grade–ish, Trevor felt, but he could still respect that. Except he didn't understand why Marty wasn't worried that Cindy would scream at a bug.

He watched Marty pull out a pen from his pocket and scribble some words on the bag. Then he held it up for her to see. Trevor couldn't hear what Marty said to her, but he saw Cindy smile wider than ever and throw her arms around him.

What in nature was going on?!

Wow, Trevor thought. Girls now LIKE it when we show them icky stuff? Good to know.

As Tad led the group down the trail, his pace began to pick up. "Kids, up here! I want to show you something!"

Trevor popped up on his toes to get a look at whatever it was that Tad wanted to show them now.

But what was up ahead was not a rock. Or a twig. Or anything vest-related.

What he saw made his stomach drop.

It was a swiftly moving river with a rickety-looking log bridge across it.

"Time for some adventure!" Tad yelled.

Trevor came to a halt.

No. No, no, no.

He knew that if he tried to cross the river using that bridge, he would—without a doubt—fall in and get sopping wet. And if he didn't fall on his own, Corey would push him in. It was just too tempting to a guy who was constantly looking for ways to humiliate seventh graders. Plus, that strange smirk Corey had given him earlier was a sure sign that humiliation was soon to follow.

Trevor had to find a way out of this.

His heart raced, and his palms turned clammy.

Think, think!

As all the kids excitedly gathered along the side of the river, eager to cross over, Trevor snuck around and rushed up to Tad. He had to try *something*. "I can't cross over this rickety bridge," he said in a low voice so no one could hear.

Tad's smile turned to a frown, and he looked almost hurt. "But this is the adventure part." He looked through the list of names on his clipboard. "What's your name?"

"Trevor Jones."

"I don't see anywhere in my notes here that you're supposed to get special treatment."

He shook his head. "No, my mom didn't make any requests. Wait. People can make special requests?!"

"Sure. I have one student who is a vegetarian and one who's"—he followed the words with his finger as he read—"an only-meat-eater." Tad looked up. "Do you have a food allergy?"

"I have a swift-water-river allergy. Is there another way to get across the river? An easier way?"

Tad pointed upriver. "Around the bend, the water's not so fast, and there's an easy rock crossing. You won't even get wet."

Trevor grinned. "Perfect."

"Are you sure you don't want to try the bridge? It'll be fun."

Trevor started backing away. "I'm afraid of heights."

"It's only two feet high. And it's nice and wide."

"I'm scared of widths, too."

Tad looked like he was trying to hold back his laughter. "We'll meet you on the other side, then."

Trevor quickly took off upriver and didn't tell Libby or Molly what he was doing. No doubt Libby would talk him out of it, explaining that crossing over would be some metaphor for conquering fears, and Molly would just roll her eyes at him. Some decisions he had to make for himself.

As he pushed his way through the brush and approached the easy rock crossing, he could hear the voices of the students crossing the river. But then their voices turned to squeals. Then laughter. Then more squeals. High-pitched squeals! What was going on?!

He hurried across the river and ran down the trail on the other side, searching for his group. When he spotted them, all he could do was drop his head.

The entire group had fallen in the river. ALL. OF. THEM.

They were splashing around, laughing and having the time of their lives. Standing on the opposite side with completely dry clothes, Trevor looked like the odd duck. (If *odd duck* meant a seventh grader who is left out by looking ridiculous in his dry clothes.)

Trevor decided right then and there to stick with the group no matter what. Surely that way he wouldn't feel humiliated.

Surely.

Corey Long

Laughing quite
a bit

1:40 p.m.

We all got sopping wet! It was EPIC! And did you
see Trevor on the OTHER side of the river? COM-
PLETELY DRY! He must have felt ridiculous being
the only dry one.

And get this . . . it ended up that the entire
group falling into the river was the best thing
that could have happened to me! Now EVERYONE has
straggly hair hanging in their eyes, and I finally
don't feel like a loser.

You know what? I'm starting to like the outdoors. Thumbs-up, nature. You rock.

Libby Gardner

Wringing out her
wet hair

1:43 p.m.

I've decided that crossing a river is a metaphor.
For going on to the next phase in life. Or crossing over your troubles and leaving them behind. Or
helping you figure out if a certain someone—I'm
not going to mention names, but let's just say his
name is, oh . . . Lorey Cong—is a good match for
you.

With everyone having scraggly hair and Corey,
er, I mean, Lorey, finally smiling and having a
good time, I might find out my answer soon enough.
Oh, who am I kidding . . . Corey is smiling! Quite
nicely, I might add. But there's still much more
to find out. Favorite color. Movie likes. Personality quirks. Weather preferences. SO MUCH!

I have a feeling all my questions will be
answered at the social tonight—the one that
Savannah is planning. Which reminds me . . .

[twirls her wet hair nervously]

I've been focusing on this Corey thing to distract me from my REAL problem—the one where I haven't yet come up with an epic idea for the Wednesday-night social. The thought of following Savannah, with her perfect party planning, is overwhelming.

How will I ever get through this without packets of emergency ranch dressing?

[narrows eyes]

I won't give up—it's time to do what I do best: scribble ideas in my sketchbook.

CHAPTER THIRTEEN

THE GROUP BLISSFULLY HIKED THROUGH THE WOODS IN sopping wet clothes. Step, squish, step, squish. And no one complained. Even Molly was almost pleasantly content since the wet clothes were keeping her from getting too hot in the sun, which kept annoyingly interacting with her. She wasn't smiling, but she wasn't snarling, either.

Tad led the group to a clearing and had everyone sit down and get comfortable. "As part of your science curriculum, we are going to study animal tracks," he explained as he held up cards showing what different animal tracks look like. "We have plenty of wildlife around here, and you'll find raccoon tracks or coyote or black bear or even possibly . . ." He paused to add some drama. "The elusive, scary-awesome grizzly bear!"

The students squirmed with delight-slash-fear.

"If that's too scary, though," Tad added, "I have an alternate activity for you. A word search. Otherwise, explore the area with your Sensitivity Buddy, and let us know if you find something!" Tad said it with a wink because there had never been a grizzly bear sighting in the camp's history. Grizzly bears didn't even live in this part of the country.

Trevor had learned his lesson from last time. *Just do what everybody else is doing.*

He looked up and saw Corey stomping toward the thick woods.

Before he could follow, he heard a voice over his shoulder. "Why aren't you wet like the rest of us?"

He whirled around to see Molly with her hands on her hips.

"I'm an idiot, of course," Trevor said.

"I think we're all going to act like idiots at some point on this trip," she said.

This made him smile. There was something about Molly, like she was always there for him, but in an accidental way. Or maybe it was on purpose? He wasn't sure. Either way, he smiled—big-time.

"Why are you smiling so big?" Molly asked.

He considered telling her that he liked how she always seemed to say the right thing, whether she meant to or not. But then he realized that sounded sort of weird. "I don't know why I'm smiling. I'm supposed to be making *you* smile." He stuck his hands in his pockets, then said, "Look, I have an idea. I'll meet you back here after this activity and give it to you then."

"Give what to me?"

He strolled off toward the woods and casually said over his shoulder, "You'll see."

It only took several long strides before he was in the woods, away from the group. After tipping over a few rocks, he found what he was looking for. A fat, squirmy potato bug. If Cindy liked icky stuff, he figured Molly would adore it.

Without even remembering that he had a fear of bugs, he stashed it in his pocket, then hurried into the forest to meet up with Corey.

Up ahead he saw Corey surveying the ground with a serious look on his face—a determined face. "Find anything yet?" Trevor asked.

Corey ignored his question as he scanned the ground, then said, "Tell me what's going on with Libby."

"What do you mean?"

"She won't even look my way, and she spends all her time jotting down notes in her notebook. Tell me the truth. Is she writing letters to another guy? Is this because of my hair?"

Trevor's stomach did a flip. This question, this moment. It was all too good. He could simply tell Corey, "Yes, she's writing letters to another guy—a guy with amazing hair," and his ego wouldn't be able to take it. He'd give up on Libby, and this would be over.

But Trevor also had that truthiness problem. "She's just writing notes about her plans for the social."

Fine. You win, truth.

Trevor couldn't help but add, "But if you knew Libby, you'd know that was normal behavior for her."

Corey stood up taller and swiped his un-gelled hair out of his face. He looked relieved. "She's making plans for the social. I like that. Now let's hunt down some bear tracks and win this competition."

"I don't think it's a game or anything," Trevor said as Corey disappeared into the woods. He quickly sped up his pace and found Corey several oak trees away, staring down at the ground. But when he looked up at Trevor, his face had lost all color.

"What. Is. THAT?" Corey pointed down at something on the ground.

Moving closer, Trevor saw that this wasn't just a little paw print. It wasn't even golden retriever big. It was huge. HUGE!

"No way!" Trevor squealed. "Is this a—"

"Bear print, and not even a regular black bear. It's a grizzly, dude!" Corey started backing away.

Trevor's mind flooded with all the wilderness facts he'd studied in an attempt to get out of this trip. Was it possible these were grizzly tracks? Do they live here? He searched and searched his brain, but he was too distracted by the frightened look on Corey's face.

"We gotta go tell Tad!" Corey said. Then he took off in a sprint as he yelled, "Grizzly bear! GRIZZLY BEAR!!"

Trevor followed him and did the same. As they approached the open area where Tad and the rest of the group was, they continued yelling and throwing their arms in the air. "Help! IT'S A GRIZZLY BEAR!"

Except, somewhere along the way, Trevor noticed that Corey had fallen behind. He wasn't with him, backing him up on their grizzly bear claim. Instead, Corey had strolled next to Libby and was chatting her up.

Tad shook his head. "Not cool, Trevor. Nature is a serious thing. Grizzlies don't even live in this part of the country."

Trevor sighed. Why was he always the odd duck? In related news, Trevor looked around and saw that everyone was gathered around Tad's backpack, eating. Why weren't they all out looking for animal tracks?

Cindy Applegate waved to Trevor and called out, "Trev, you should've stayed behind like the rest of us. The alternate activity was a word search and M&M'S! You're no grizzly bear hunter!"

All the girls around her started laughing. Then everyone started. Trevor was pretty sure that even some squirrels nearby were laughing.

So rude.

When the laughter died down, Trevor quietly approached Molly. At least he had something to give her that would make her smile, and he could redeem this moment in some way. "Hey, Molly," he whispered. "I found this for you." Trevor reached into his pocket and pulled out her surprise.

Molly looked down at his hand, and her eyes grew big.

"Wait. You *don't* like bugs? I'm confused." Trevor just couldn't seem to catch a break.

Molly scrunched up her face. "If the bug had been wiggling and alive, it would've been gross. But a dead bug?" She looked up, her eyes showing a sparkle. "It's awesome."

He couldn't believe that ignoring his fear of bugs worked out. More than that, Molly Decker almost smiled.

Almost.

Corey Long

Kicking dirt,
covering up the
bear print

2:10 p.m.

OF COURSE I'm going to mess with Trevor on this hike. That's why I faked the grizzly bear sighting. It happened to me last year when someone in my group faked a Bigfoot sighting. It was pretty rude, man. So I'm just passing it along—circle of life—type stuff. And that's nature, if you think about it. So technically, I should be getting extra credit for that grizzly bear stunt with Trevor.

At least it will impress my brother when I tell him. Not that I see him all too often since he's usually involved in an after-school activity.

It's called DETENTION.

And I have to find a way to go out in style. I mean, this is my last week at Westside Middle School. Only a few days left to leave an impression.

I guess impressing the other kids is what I did best at this school. It's really the only thing I tried hard at.

Molly Decker

Plucking petals
off a flower

2:12 p.m.

Sure, I love dead bugs. But I do not love marsh-mallows; I'm going to put that out there right up front.

Things that decay are COOL. That bug Trevor gave me? It decays. Cool.

Apples? They decay. Also cool.

But marshmallows? No decaying. That's creepy. They just hang around and never go away, like a weird cousin or something.

Gosh, I'm really talkative right now.

It's from nerves. Because . . . here's the deal. I need to find a time to tell Trevor my news. Even though he shouldn't be shocked by it. I mean, I came to this school after being trans-ferred from several other schools, all because my dad keeps getting moved around.

And Dad is getting moved to another school again. But this time it's for a promotion.

The job is far away, so that means . . .

[takes a deep breath]

135

. . . this week will probably be the last time I'll ever see Trevor.

Needless to say, I'm not talking to my dad right now.

I don't even want to imagine how Trevor will take the news.

So right now I'm just going to focus on this dead bug.

CHAPTER FOURTEEN

THE DAY HAD BEEN FULL OF ACTIVITY—HIKING, MORE hiking, and watching Tad clean off his vest. But the sun was falling, and that meant it was time for dinner. Mr. Skeely rang the bell, and the students scampered and skittered, descending on the dining room like an army of ants. *Hungry* ants.

"Hold up!" Mr. Skeely held up his giant folktale palm. "Marty was first last time. So the last person last time will go first this time."

Somehow that all happened to make sense, and the entire school turned around to look at Cindy. She had just busted through the doors.

"I'M HERE. I MADE IT!" She strutted right up in front of Marty.

"Where were you?" he whispered over her shoulder.

"Feeding Lucy," she said out of the side of her mouth. "She seemed happy that your bag said *fancy*, so I set it down and rushed out, making sure she didn't follow me down here." Cindy grabbed her plate, looked left and right to make sure no one else was listening, and turned to him. "It wasn't easy, though—I even formed a sweat bead. Oh my goodness, is my hair okay?"

Marty wasn't sure what to say, since her hair always looked okay. "It always looks okay."

"Aww, that's sweet!" She beamed.

He'd said the right thing.

But during this sweet conversation in which Marty was saying all the right things, Cindy—having not memorized Skeely's New & Improved Flowchart—accidentally flowed in the wrong direction. Marty didn't even realize it.

Within mere moments, Cindy had caused a full-school pileup.

In the chaos, Trevor noticed Libby had kept her cool and was still taking notes and measurements to get prepared for the social. "You sure are focused," Trevor said to her.

She nodded and quickly measured a table. "Some ideas are coming to me. They're *vague* ideas, but they're ideas.

Okay, I have *one* idea." She looked up and lifted a brow. "But more importantly, how did things go with Corey today? Is he boyfriend material? I need your thoughts on this, Trev."

He didn't have any—not just yet. It was possible that Corey had tricked him with the grizzly bear track. But he couldn't prove that. And after thinking it through, he realized Corey hadn't actually done anything horrible to him that day. But he hadn't gone through a night yet, so his opinion was still in the forming stage.

"I'll let you know in the morning, Lib. You know . . . if I'm alive."

She smirked at him. "You know how you'll stay alive?"

There was a twinkle in her eye. And he needed to get

to the bottom of that twinkle. (If twinkles have bottoms, that is.) "How?"

"By focusing on Molly Decker and making that girl smile." She winked at him. "That way you'll keep your mind busy, and your body won't die. That sounded weird, but you know what I mean."

He nodded as he watched Libby skip around helping people who were still on the floor because of Cindy's pileup.

"LISTEN UP!" Skeely howled. "No one is flowing in the right direction. Yes, it is Cindy's fault, but she has apologized and blamed it on the fact that she is so short. I have no idea what it's like to be short, so I can't even imagine how challenging her life must be. But I must add that someone—one person in particular—snatched a fork before grabbing a napkin. This has turned into a disaster. And now you are to eat your meal in silence. No talking!"

Who was the idiot who grabbed a fork first? Trevor thought.

Silence fell over the room. All you could hear was the scraping of wood chairs against the wood floors as everyone sat down to eat their Tuna Casserole Surprise in silence.

Whew. At least I'm not the one who caused us to get in trouble, Trevor thought.

But that's when he looked down at his fork. Suddenly

he remembered . . . *he* had grabbed a fork first. Trevor looked to his right to see that Skeely was eyeballing him from across the room.

I'm the idiot. Should've seen that one coming.

But then when he looked to his left, he saw Molly, three tables down, sneaking glances at him. Her hand covered her mouth, and her shoulders lifted up and down.

Molly was laughing?

She then coughed and turned away.

But Molly's almost-giggle did not go unnoticed. Trevor now knew there was a possible way to get Molly to smile huge. All that was required was doing something embarrassing in front of everyone.

Easy, Trevor thought. Slam dunk.

Cindy Applegate

Super grumpy

6:35 p.m.

Yeah, it's super neat and all that the Jolly Green Giant didn't get me in trouble for causing that all-school pileup. But that doesn't mean my life hasn't turned into a DISASTER.

I tried to eat my Tuna Casserole Surprise next to Savannah Maxwell, but she glared at me and left the table. So if you're following along, that means she left me there ALL ALONE. True, there were seven other people at the table, but essentially I was left alone in the wilderness to fend for myself.

I kept promising her that I'd get back to the room as soon as possible to decorate her bed, but there's just so much programming at this camp that they don't give you a moment to breathe or rest or sneak food to a cat.

I'm just glad I have Lucy to cuddle up with. She's making this nightmare tolerable with all her cuteness. Everyone should pack a stowaway kitty. I highly recommend it.

CHAPTER FIFTEEN

THE STUDENTS WERE GIVEN A FEW MINUTES TO RUSH back to their cabins to get ready for the evening social. When Libby entered the cabin, she saw Savannah calmly gathering party items.

"So . . ." Libby said as she casually folded and refolded the cuff on her sleeve, ". . . do you need any help tonight?"

"Nope." Savannah packed and stacked and twirled around to face her. "All ready. It should be a blast." As she strutted out of the cabin, she glanced back over her shoulder and said, "Can't wait to see what you have planned, Libby. And get my bed decorated, Cindy!"

"I'm on it—I promise!" Cindy said while upside-down, looking under a bed.

Libby flopped down on her bed. She stared up at the bottom of the top bunk, hoping some answers were hidden there. She had an idea for her social, but what if it wasn't nearly as sparkly as what Savannah had planned? She sighed and said, "Cindy, why are you staring under my bed and not decorating Savannah's?"

She popped her head up next to Libby. "Me? I'm not looking for anything. But I was just wondering . . . have you seen any skunks in our cabin?"

Libby sat up straight and grabbed her blanket. "Skunks? In here?!"

"Calm down. There are no skunks *in* our cabin, of course." Cindy nervously twirled her hair. She realized that having Lucy in the cabin could cause big trouble. As much as she wanted to have her kitty nearby, she was going to have to put her bedding and food outside behind the cabin. As long as there was fancy food nearby, Lucy wouldn't travel far.

The other girls rushed into the cabin, flittering about as they changed their clothes and quickly got ready for the social, then rushed back out in a flurry. Cindy looked around and realized she was left with only Libby—who was staring at a list in her notebook—and Molly, who was staring down at her boots.

"What is wrong with you people? There's a fantastic social about to start." Cindy pointed to the door. "Why aren't you girls rushing down there?"

Molly folded her arms. "Anything with the word *social* in it is something I'd like to stay far away from. What's *your* excuse?"

"I promised Savannah I'd decorate her bed. I have to get that done first." Cindy then turned to face Libby. "Why aren't you heading down there, Ms. Class President?"

Libby sighed. "I'm sure Savannah has planned something adorable and extravagant, and there's no way I'll be able to follow anything she does."

"Are you kidding?" Molly said as she marched up to Libby. "I saw her putting up the decorations earlier. They're ridiculous. Trust me, you have nothing to worry about. Come on." Molly then grabbed Libby by the arm and pulled her out of the cabin.

"Toodles!" Cindy called out after them as they headed down the trail, Molly dragging Libby alongside her.

Perfect, Cindy thought. Now I can get Lucy all super comfy in her new bed outside and still have time to decorate Savannah's bed!

But by the time she had moved Lucy's bed outside and "fancified" it with beautiful foliage and flowers and ribbons, she'd run out of time. She had to put off decorating Savannah's bed until later—yet again.

Libby and Molly arrived in the dining hall, and Libby's mouth dropped.

"See? I told you," Molly said. "It's ridiculous, right?"

"These are all my ideas. A corner for Pictionary, pin the tail on the bear, a Jenga tournament. These are all things I'd thought of! I mean, I had a list of *a lot* of things in my head, but I can't believe she thought of these, too!"

Molly shrugged. "No offense, but they're pretty bad ideas. Don't you think it's kind of cool that Savannah is the one who has to take credit for this dumb party?"

Libby's eyes teared up. "I know you're being nice, but it also kind of hurts."

Molly patted Libby on the shoulder. "You'll come up with something better. You always do, Libby. I've never met someone with so many problem-solving skills. Seriously, you're ready to run Congress or something."

She turned to Molly, wiping a tear from her eye. "Thanks. That's probably the nicest thing you've ever said to me. It's interesting how you can say something sort of mean and then follow it up with something sort of wonderful." She patted Molly's shoulder. "I like that about you."

Molly bit at her lip because she didn't like the feeling welling up inside her. Maybe Trevor wasn't the only one she was going to miss at this school. She looked down at the floor and said, "I'm going to the bathroom." Then she bolted out of there before she showed any more stupid emotions.

But just as she got to the door, she heard, "Molly! I'm glad you liked that dead potato bug." It was Trevor.

"Yeah, I liked it."

He motioned toward the party. "Wanna go play Pictionary with me?"

She realized they were away from the group. No one could hear them. It would be the perfect time to tell him she was moving. So she took a deep breath and looked up at him. "I have something I need to tell you."

"Before or after Pictionary?"

"Now."

He stepped closer to her and smiled. The fact that Molly wanted to talk about something meant that she was softening up. Sharing emotions. Not being so miserable! And that meant, of course, that he was that much closer to getting her to smile like crazy. "Tell me anything. Just lay it on me!"

But Molly studied his face—his smile, his bright eyes.

It was obvious he thought she was about to say something good.

Not something devastating.

There was a whole other day left at Whispering Pines. So Molly decided now was not the time. Ruining this trip was never what she intended to do.

She fidgeted with her jacket. "Let's do pin the tail on the bear instead. It might actually be fun."

Trevor's eyes grew big. "Really? That's so positive of you!"

She shrugged. "I'll give it a shot." The two of them headed back into the dining hall, and that's when they saw Libby and Savannah in the corner talking.

Voices were raised.

Hands were flying.

Oh, no, Trevor thought. Whenever Libby's hands flail like that, it means things are about to fall apart.

Libby Gardner

Outside the dining
hall, super annoyed

8:40 p.m.

ALL I asked her was how she figured out what I was planning, and she went all berserk, saying there are LOTS of ideas and it's not like she stole them.

I told her I never accused her of stealing them and blah, blah, blah . . . we ended the conversation in a dare. That's probably normal between two class presidents, right?

[laughs nervously]

[clears throat]

She dared me to give a better party than she did.

WHAT ARE WE, FIVE?

I didn't tell her that I'd already dared myself to throw a better party. Except it isn't going to be easy, because the only idea of mine she DIDN'T think of was Literary Limbo. It was the only one left on my list.

But now I'm wondering if that idea is lame,

too. I know Molly thinks that I'll come up with something else amazing, but I've been trying to do everything possible to loosen up my creative side.

I've taken a long shower.

Walked by myself in the woods.

Even did a headstand.

But nothing—no unique ideas have jostled out!

[looks down]

I guess it should make me feel better that everyone seemed to have a decent enough time at Savannah's social tonight. If I'd gone first, they would've been happy at MY social.

Though, I have to admit . . . they were having a decent time but not a GREAT time.

[looks up, twinkle in her eye]

Which means there's a chance that I could come up with something better. So I need to get going. Time for another headstand!

Savannah Maxwell

Fluffing and refluffing her hair

8:43 p.m.

I'm not sure about that Libby girl. She's never done anything for ME. It's like she thinks she can pull off this whole "Amazing Class President" thing without even shadowing me and asking for advice or borrowing clothes. This entire year, she's been making decisions all by herself. I'm tired of it!!

So, yes. I challenged her to a dare. I figured it was the proper way to handle the situation.

[checks her fingernails]

I'm sophisticated like that. Wow, these nails are chipped. Nice weather is so brutal on the nails sometimes.

I'll get Cindy to touch them up. THAT girl knows how to be a shadow. It's possible I'll take her on as a protégé. But I'll wait to see how my bed decorations turned out first.

Miss Plimp

Drumming her
fingers on her
clipboard

8:45 p.m.

I'm not sure I'd call Savannah's party a success. She made a lot of safe choices. Pictionary? Yes. Jenga? Sure. All good ideas, but they are the obvious ones. I guess I was just hoping for a twist. Like the kind you find in good movies. Or interesting food.

Something unusual!

I studied the students, and there were some smiles, but I recorded no one laughing out loud or even grinning widely. So I'll be looking forward to what Libby has in store for us tomorrow night.

Let's hope she can figure out a twist.

CHAPTER SIXTEEN

THE STUDENTS GATHERED AROUND THE ROARING FIRE AS Tad and Miss Plimp happily greeted them and said things with exclamation points.

"Get warm!"

"Let's have fun!!"

"There will be s'mores!!!"

"Time for campfire songs!!!!"

Tad stood up and got the students' attention. "It's time to sing a camp favorite, 'On Top of Spaghetti'!" The lyrics were highly tolerable to a group of middle school students, and within just a couple of lines, they were all belting out the words.

On top of spaghetti,
all covered with cheese,
I lost my poor meatball,
when somebody sneezed.
It rolled off the table,
and onto the floor,
and then my poor meatball,
rolled out of the door. . . .

When the class got to the second round of the song, everyone—even Corey—was up on their feet, singing and waving their hands around wildly.

Vice Principal Decker was on the outside of the group, waving his hands around in support. Trevor couldn't help but jump up and join in, too.

And strangely enough, he found himself having fun.

But when he glanced over at Molly, she had her hoodie pulled tight around her head. No smile, no laugh. No reaction at all, actually. It was almost as if she didn't even care what was going on around her.

Something's wrong, Trevor thought. She's not usually in THIS bad of a mood.

As soon as the singing was over, Miss Plimp announced

it was time to cook up s'mores. The students all scattered in different lines to pick up their ingredients, but Trevor lingered, looking for Molly.

He didn't have to look very hard. Molly had already spotted him. "Come over here," she said as she motioned for him to follow her to the side.

She plopped down on a log bench and patted the spot next to her. "Sit down. We need to talk."

Trevor cautiously sat down. This was all pretty weird. He couldn't remember a time when Molly had initiated a conversation. And certainly not one that involved the sentence *We need to talk*. Trevor glanced her way. "What's wrong? Was it that spaghetti song?"

"No."

"My voice. You hate my singing voice."

"No, Trevor."

"When I stood up and waved my hands around, I looked like a Muppet. Is that it?"

She smirked. "No."

"A *dorky* Muppet?"

She laughed, then quickly coughed to cover it up.

"Aha! I almost made you smile, Molly Decker! This quest of mine may be more difficult than *The Hobbit*, but I *will* succeed."

Molly looked over at him and flinched when she saw his face.

Excitement.

He was truly excited about making her smile.

It hit her that she had never had a friend like Trevor before. And maybe she never would again. So the thought of telling him she was moving away hurt her insides more than she could bear.

"So . . . what'd you need to talk to me about?" he asked.

Molly pulled her hoodie over her head. "It's true—you looked like a Muppet."

"You pulled me over here to tell me that?"

"No." Then she jumped up and ran off without saying another word.

For the rest of the campfire, Molly sat on the opposite side of the group from Trevor. With her hoodie pulled tight, he couldn't even see a silhouette of her face.

"What did I do wrong?" Trevor grumbled to himself as he roasted a marshmallow. *This is the second time she's told me we need to talk, but she won't talk! What should I say to her . . . aww, dang it.*

He'd burned his marshmallow, so he tossed it into the

fire. He didn't even stay to watch it turn into a molten lava burst of marshmallow awesome. Instead, he sat back down on a log, sank his chin into his palm, and thought through all the possible ways he could make Molly happy again.

The problem was that he couldn't think of a way—not a single idea.

"Time for a ghost story!" Miss Plimp announced.

There were equal amounts of groans and squeals of excitement. Apparently, eagerness to hear a ghost story ran at about 50 percent. Trevor was in the eager category because he never actually found ghost stories to be scary.

There were always plot holes.

"I have a ghost story!" Corey jumped up on a log and stuck a flashlight under his chin. "Listen up, everyone. . . ."

Trevor covered his face with his hands. *Oh, no. If anyone can actually make a ghost story terrifying, it would be Corey.*

With a low and raspy voice, Corey began. "It was on a night just like tonight. . . ."

The students ooooohed and squirmed as they settled in for the story.

Corey squinted his eyes to increase the tension. "A man named One-Armed William—"

"Don't you mean Willy?" someone called out.

"William. Willy. Whatever! Here's the story. . . ." Back to tension-squinting. "Years ago, he escaped from the local maximum-security jail—"

A question came from the audience. "What was he in jail for?"

Then another. "Where exactly was the jail located?"

And yet another. "How could William escape a maximum-security jail if he had only one arm?"

Trevor couldn't help but grin.

Plot holes.

Even in the dark, Corey's angry red face was visible. "You guys *really* need his entire backstory?" He folded his arms and thought for a moment. "Fine. Here's your back-story. One-Armed William was the son of a gold miner, and he lost his arm at the tender age of ten years old in a tragic gold-mining incident that involved an explosion that killed everyone in his family, so he grew up with a lot of resentment, and that's why he turned to a life of crime that involved him exploding buildings for fun, which was why he was arrested when he was found trying to place a stick of dynamite in the mayor's bathroom, except no one realized that he'd smuggled one last piece of dynamite into the jail, and on his third day, he blew up his cell-room floor and crawled through the sewer system until he finally reached safety"—Corey took a deep breath and pointed at a hole in the ground—"right here on this very spot."

The group gasped.

Trevor went back to covering his face. *No. Way. The guy is filling in plot points, and they almost make sense!*

Corey raised an eyebrow, feeling confident that he had succeeded in scaring everyone. But not just everyone . . . *Trevor*. His goal was to prepare Trevor for what was about to happen that night: the Haunting of Cabin Thirteen.

Corey put the finishing touch on his story. "So now, One-Armed Willy—"

"William!"

Corey grunted. "One-Armed *William* haunts the grounds of Camp Whispering Pines every night, trying to get revenge."

"Wait, bro," Marty interrupted. "If he haunts, then he's a ghost. But you never said he died."

Corey slapped his forehead. "Fine. He died in an unfortunate dining hall incident involving some undercooked eggs. So now he wanders the campground, super upset about that bad breakfast with an arm that's a spiky ball and chain."

Yet again, more audience questions and concerns.

"But you never mentioned a ball and chain!"

"And shouldn't it be a hook?"

"Yeah, all ghost stories have a guy with a hook."

"Or maybe he has a rifle for an arm."

"Or a chain saw!"

"Oh, I know! His arm shoots out spears, but they're rainbow spears that smell like strawberries!!"

The last suggestion came from Cindy Applegate.

"Naw, naw!" Corey waved his arms around, looking very frustrated. "You guys are missing the point. What I'm saying is that you may hear a strange clanging sound at your window tonight, and it's probably One-Armed William getting revenge for his fatal pancake breakfast."

"EGGS!"

A small smile formed on Trevor's face. Even though Corey had come close to scaring him, he'd introduced the ball-and-chain detail far too late in the story for the plot to ring true.

Trevor wasn't scared one bit.

As the students were dismissed back to their cabins, Trevor headed off down the trail with a big grin on his face.

But he didn't realize that Corey was watching his every move.

Corey Long

Looking quite
pleased with
himself

9:32 p.m.

Did you see that grin? People ALWAYS grin when they're super scared. I know I do.

So I have a lot of prep work to do. That whole thing about William having a spiky ball and chain was just made up on the spot, so now I gotta go find something that replicates the sound of a ghost angrily hitting a spiky ball on a window.

I could use a ball with spikes all over it!

Oh, wait. I don't have one. I'll just have to search for some tin cans to bang together.

[nods as he thinks this over]

This idea is definitely going to work.

Especially since Trevor is already halfway to terrified.

It's time I pay the haunting forward. Last year, Luke Lawson ran a zip line outside my cabin and hung some clothes and sticks together to look like a skeleton and pulled it into my window.

I screeched like an owl. Also—and don't use

this for the final edit—I cried for my dad to come save me.

My dad doesn't even live in this state.

So it's taken me a full year to carefully rebuild my reputation back up to where I am now—the pinnacle of popularity.

[tosses his bangs out of his face]

I'm a survivor, man.

CHAPTER SEVENTEEN

THE TRAIL BETWEEN THE CABINS AND THE BATHROOMS was lit up with all the students' flashlights as they made their final attempts at hygiene. They hustled to and from the bathroom with their lights bouncing around, looking like a highway in a bustling city.

As Trevor walked along with his toothbrush hanging from the corner of his mouth, he immediately recognized the beam of Molly's flashlight heading toward him. It was a blue light.

She marched right up to him and stuck the light in his face. "I want you to stop trying to make me smile."

He gently pushed the light away. "Why?"

"You're ruining this trip."

Trevor was confused. He'd decided to willingly come on

this trip because of *her*. And now this? "I thought you said you were excited I was going to be on this trip."

She dipped her head and looked down. "I like you being the way you usually are—the friend who hangs with me when I'm complaining about something, maybe even joins in. But all this turning me into some Smiling Monster is just lame."

"I'm sorry? I guess?" He really didn't know if he was supposed to be sorry or what. He just knew her being mad was not the goal of the Molly Project.

In the light—or lack of—Trevor could see just the outline of her face, and he was almost certain he saw a tear form. A tear? From Molly?

He put his hand on her shoulder. "Are you okay?"

"Yep," she said, then pursed her lips.

"You sure everything's all right?"

No response.

"Blink once for yes. Twice for no," he instructed.

She blinked twice.

Something *was* going on! What could it be? "Do you want to talk about it?"

Molly turned to him, her lips still pursed, then blinked twice. Two very obvious blinks.

Nope, she didn't want to talk about it. Not one bit.

Molly aimed her blue flashlight down the trail, headed off to her cabin, and didn't look back.

Trevor settled into his lower bunk bed, while Marty was above him, clutching his favorite camouflage Snuggie blanket. He wouldn't call it a Snuggie, but really that's what it was.

The other boys were quietly reading, and Mr. Applegate was already snoring.

Trevor decided this would be a good time to get advice from Marty. But not school advice this time. Girl advice. "Hey, Marty," Trevor whispered up at the mattress ceiling above his head.

"Yeah?"

"Could you give me some advice?"

"Of course. I'm a pro. Do you need to know how to whittle something?"

"No."

"How to collect rainwater in the wilderness?"

"Um, nope."

"Make a raft out of twigs in case you're stranded?"

"Maybe later, but right now I have a question about . . . girls."

Marty scrunched his face up. This was not a topic he

was used to talking about, especially in a semipublic way like this. Getting Cindy to like him had been an uphill battle. She was a complicated girl. But he figured he'd give girl advice a shot. "Ask away. I'll do my best."

Trevor took a deep breath, then let his question flow. "What do you do if a girl seems to like you, but when you try to make her smile, she likes it at first but then she decides she doesn't like it, and then there's some problem that seems to be making her upset, and she says she doesn't want to talk about it, and it's possible there was a tear in her eye, and then she runs off with her blue light? What do I do? I mean, asking for a friend."

Marty was a little stumped. Not by the "asking for a friend" part—he knew Trevor was talking about Molly—but by the part about what to do. When it came to girls, he really needed an instruction manual. One of those easy ones like in the LEGO sets for ages four to seven.

Marty shrugged and took a guess. "If a girl says everything is all right but there's a tear in her eye . . . it probably isn't all right. So figure out what's wrong. That's all I know to do."

It was simple advice. Trevor was relieved that the Molly Project wasn't over—it had just changed direction. Enough with getting her to smile. Trevor needed to find out what or *who* was bothering Molly. "You're brilliant, Marty."

"Thanks," he said, hoping it was true. He grabbed an extra set of earplugs and dropped them down to Trevor. "Wear these. The snoring could get epic tonight."

"Won't all the other guys wake up?" he whispered.

"I gave a pair to everyone. And Mr. Applegate won't hear a thing with all his own snoring."

Trevor smiled. "Good night."

"Good night," Marty said.

And with that, Trevor went right to sleep, completely unaware that One-Armed William had come to pay a visit.

Corey Long

Fuming

10:17 p.m.

I don't get it! I DON'T GET IT!!

I saw Trevor's frightened grin after my ghost story. That dude was perfectly prepared for an epic haunting.

So why didn't he budge? Why didn't ANYONE budge?!

[paces back and forth]

My plan was foolproof. I told my chaperone I had to go to the bathroom, and I left my cabin at 9:58.

I grabbed a couple of tin cans from the recycling bin. Then I stood on my tiptoes to peer into the cabin. They were all asleep.

Smooth sailing, right? WRONG.

I clanged the cans together and made woo-ing sounds, like One-Armed William would've done.

But no matter how much I clanged or how much I woo-ed, NOTHING. No one woke up, not even Trevor. All I could hear was Mr. Applegate's snoring. How did they all sleep through that?

So all this explains why I got mad and tried to grab a rock, but then I tripped and landed in a berry bush, and now my clothes are stained with red berry juice, and some of it landed in my hair, and it won't come out and, man, I REALLY DON'T WANT TO TALK ABOUT THIS ANYMORE.

[storms off]

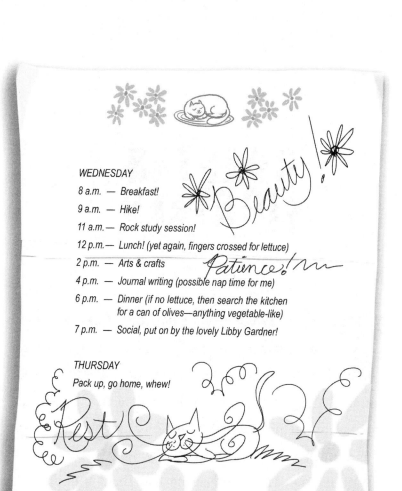

WEDNESDAY

8 a.m. — Breakfast!

9 a.m. — Hike!

11 a.m.— Rock study session!

12 p.m.— Lunch! (yet again, fingers crossed for lettuce)

2 p.m. — Arts & crafts

4 p.m. — Journal writing (possible nap time for me)

6 p.m. — Dinner (if no lettuce, then search the kitchen for a can of olives—anything vegetable-like)

7 p.m. — Social, put on by the lovely Libby Gardner!

THURSDAY

Pack up, go home, whew!

Beauty!

Patience!

Rest

CHAPTER EIGHTEEN

THE NEXT DAY WAS THEIR FINAL HIKE. COREY LINGERED behind, staying at the back of the group, dealing with his sour mood. Trevor, on the other hand, bounced along the trail, looking forward to all the day's events. He was invigorated by his great night's sleep that didn't involve any appearances by ghosts whatsoever. Except for the strange dream he had about a ghost who was in a tin can band. So much clanging. And wooing. But he shook off the dream and happily headed down the trail.

Up ahead of him, he noticed Libby with a stressed look on her face.

He briskly hiked up next to her. "What's wrong?"

"Everything."

"I don't think it's statistically possible for *everything* to be wrong, Lib."

"First, there's this." She handed him a crumpled note.

Libby looked overwhelmed. "I haven't gotten all the answers on my *Pop Psychology* quiz, so I have no idea how to answer him. And worse?" Libby frantically flipped through papers on her clipboard. "I have to come up with something completely new for tonight's social. Everyone will think I stole the ideas from Savannah."

"Relax. It's a social. People can wander around, talk, eat some food. You don't have to plan everything."

Libby's eyes grew huge. "You mean, don't plan *anything*? Not even Literary Limbo?"

"That's not exactly—"

"Whoa. Just let people *be* . . . like in nature." She tapped her chin as she considered this. "Oh my gosh, that even has a wilderness theme!"

Trevor worried he'd sent her down the wrong path. "Um, don't you want to plan *one* event? You still have the stick for limbo."

Libby threw her hands in the air, like she'd just crossed the finish line of a marathon. "No plan—*that's* my plan!" She paced around for a moment, a large grin on her face, and finally calmed down enough to take a break and sit down next to a tree.

Libby looked up at him and said, "Maybe I put too much thought into things. I'm too rigid. Am I the only seventh grader who has a label maker at the top of her Christmas list?"

"Of course you are."

She pressed her lips together. "I appreciate your honesty."

After a weird silence, Libby lifted her chin and said,

"Enough about me. Let's figure *you* out." When Libby was exhausted by her own problems, she often found solving *other* people's problems to be downright relaxing.

"Me?!" His voice cracked.

"The Molly Project. It seems to be having a big impact on you—it's like you're changing or something."

"Changing? Me?" He glanced down at his hands, flipping them over to make sure he wasn't turning werewolf.

"You've been following Molly around trying to make her smile, you're singing campfire songs like a contestant on a reality show, and you picked up a BUG." She narrowed her eyes. "Who *are* you?"

He waved her off. "Stop. It's nothing."

She folded her arms the way she did when she was about to get a little judge-y. "You know, if I didn't think you were doing all that to keep your mind off Corey, I might think that you like Molly."

"Like?!" he yelped.

"Yep. Like-like."

"Nah, I'm just being friendly." Trevor needed to change the subject quick. And he knew exactly what would get her to stop questioning him about Molly. "Speaking of like-like, what's your decision on Corey?"

She flipped over a few pages on her clipboard. "I'm still

trying to finish up this pro-con chart. I'm not sure how to get the answers to some of these questions."

He grabbed the list from her, read it over, and looked up. "You need to know whether he prefers toothpaste that's spearmint or winter mint?"

"A guy who chooses spearmint is not serious about finding a girlfriend. Spearmint just tastes like gum . . . it doesn't belong in a mouth-hygiene routine. But since you're Corey's hiking partner, can you help me out with a few of these? I want to make my decision tonight at the social, around eight p.m. When I'm on deadline, I make great decisions."

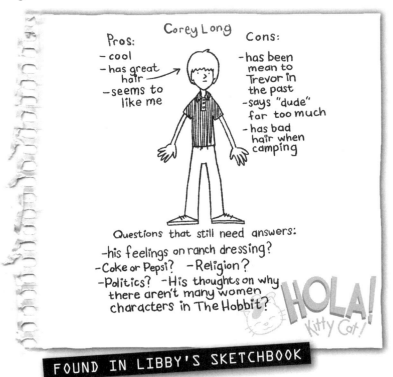

Corey Long

Pros:
- cool
- has great hair
- seems to like me

Cons:
- has been mean to Trevor in the past
- says "dude" far too much
- has bad hair when camping

Questions that still need answers:
- his feelings on ranch dressing?
- Coke or Pepsi? - Religion?
- Politics? - His thoughts on why there aren't many women characters in The Hobbit?

HOLA! Kitty Cat!

FOUND IN LIBBY'S SKETCHBOOK

Trevor wasn't sure how he could get Corey to answer some of these. How could he simply walk up to him and suddenly have a deep conversation about salad dressing?

He patted Libby on the back. "Don't worry. I'll find out all these answers."

But first Trevor had to find the guts to get all these answers—guts he didn't have at the moment.

Corey Long

Unusually nervous

11:05 a.m.

Time is running out for me, man. I told my brother I'd make him proud and pull pranks that would uphold the family name.

So far, I've failed.

That grizzly bear footprint hoax fell a little flat.

The campfire ghost story didn't seem to scare anyone. And the haunting of Cabin Thirteen only seemed to make them sleep more soundly.

It's time to turn this ship around.

And by ship, I mean "SUCCESSFUL pranks I'm going to pull on Trevor."

Today will go down in Prank-Victim History.

CHAPTER NINETEEN

COREY DIDN'T SEE ANY OTHER CHOICE. **H**E HAD TO TURN to some foolproof pranks. He also referred to them as "things I looked up on the Internet."

The rest of the afternoon consisted of studying rocks, sketching plants in their journals, and doing an arts and crafts project where the students made a necklace entirely out of things found in the woods. And then there was one bathroom break.

But Corey had other plans . . . three pranks that simply couldn't fail. These had taken some serious time to research, and he was glad he'd looked them up—for emergencies. Because here he was, in the depths of a prank emergency.

The "Tabasco in the Drink" Trick

Somehow it was Cindy who grabbed the pranked cup, not Trevor. Corey felt a little bad about that. But not *very* bad. Because the next prank would work for sure.

(Tobasco)

The "Pancake Syrup on Your Head" Trick

Yet again, Corey accidentally pulled his prank on someone other than Trevor. But he had one final trick up his sleeve.

Next up was a scheduled bathroom

break. Corey got in line right in front of Trevor. He would get it all set up, Trevor would come in after him, and *whammo!* Prank pulled on the correct person!

PRANK #3

The Never Fails "Icy Hot on the Toilet Seat" Trick

(It was truly unfortunate timing that Trevor let Marty cut in line.)

Corey didn't know Trevor had such ninja skills. How did he evade *every single* prank he'd set up?

It hit him that there was only one way to pull an epic prank on Trevor.

He had to get him completely alone.

Jordan Rossi

Quivering outside
the boys' bathroom

4:45 p.m.

D-did you see him? Marty—he had steam coming out of, well . . . everywhere. Anger steam.

He is one scary dude.

But when I think about it, he hasn't been scary toward me this whole time.

[scratches head]

Maybe I need to rethink this.

Cindy Applegate

All in a kerfuffle

4:48 p.m.

DO NOT DRINK THE JUICE. It's salsa flavored. But also smoky flavored. It's weird. It certainly wasn't fruit flavored like our Viking cafeteria manager told us it would be.

Which reminds me that there is no way we will find fancy enough food for Lucy in that cafeteria. And that also reminds me that I haven't seen much of Lucy lately. But I did see a pile of feathers near my cabin door. Surely she's not attacking birds or something. And she has also pushed away all the ribbons and lace I put on her bed. Now it's just leaves and twigs.

Is it possible Lucy has gone . . . WILD?

[shakes her head in disbelief]

No, I can't accept that. As soon as I find some fancy smoked salmon with lemon zest and a well-fitted cashmere sweater, she'll be back to normal in no time.

I know my skunk—CAT, I mean cat!

Oh, boy.

Libby Gardner

Super fidgety

6:30 p.m.

Absolutely! I'm totally ready for the social. Trevor's suggestion to just let things happen naturally was pretty brilliant.

But I did go ahead and make a sign for the party theme since ALL parties need a theme.

Oh, and I also went ahead and created a scavenger hunt activity. No biggie; it's simple. It's just that the Over Planner in me felt left out, and sometimes I have no control over my inner Over Planner.

Gosh, that made no sense.

Anyway, I just happened to have the perfect card-stock paper packed in my bag so I could write down scavenger hunt clues.

This may turn out to be the best unplanned party I've ever planned!

Wow, I'm really not making sense.

CHAPTER TWENTY

THE STUDENTS GATHERED IN THE DINING HALL FOR the trip's final social event. Libby stepped on a chair and held up Miss Plimp's megaphone. "Our first activity is a nature scavenger hunt for objects found nearby. Grab your Sensitivity Buddy to find your object, and meet back here!"

Miss Plimp cupped her hand around her mouth to form her own megaphone and called out, "What's planned after that, Libby?"

Libby was a little nervous to give her answer, but she took a deep breath and stood up a little straighter. "I have nothing planned, Miss Plimp."

Murmurs and whispers rippled through the group. The students had attended countless school parties that Libby

185

had been in charge of, and all were planned down to the millisecond. So this "I have nothing planned" statement was practically front-page news.

But she had been inspired by nature, along with Trevor's suggestion to "do nothing." Which led to her idea for a theme.

It took a little brainstorming for her to come up with the winning one.

party theme ideas:

Float... like a breeze!
Skip... like a stone!
Waddle... like a duck!
☆ Meander... like a stream! ☆

HOLA!
Kitty Cat!

Libby ignored the whispering and continued. "The theme of this party is . . ." She paused to create a dramatic moment. "Meander . . . like a stream!"

It took a moment for this idea to sink in. During the awkward silence, Libby added, "We're in nature. Just act naturally. Do whatever you want."

The concerned faces turned to relief, and happy murmurs filled the room. Miss Plimp joined Libby on the chair, teetering as she took her megaphone to speak. The room silenced as they waited to hear Miss Plimp's reaction. The seventh grade class president not planning anything for the social would be disappointing to a counselor.

But Miss Plimp smirked and said, "A wilderness theme . . . I like it."

Libby let out a sigh of relief and hopped off the chair.

Trevor was on the side of the room and flashed Libby a quick thumbs-up.

"Head off with your buddy to find your object," Miss Plimp said. "I'll be listening for compliments!"

The students quickly skittered away in pairs to hunt down their objects.

Trevor stared at his card.

Enjoy your "Meander" Scavenger Hunt! Please find something BLUE

TREVOR'S SCAVENGER HUNT CARD

Corey suddenly appeared and snatched the card from him. "Easy. I got this." He charged off through the dining hall, out the doors, and toward the woods.

"I thought we were supposed to look around here!" Trevor called out after him.

But Corey was already hauling it into the woods.

Trevor quickly double knotted his shoes and rushed off after him. "Whoa. Corey, hold up!"

Corey didn't slow down, so Trevor broke out into a hike-jog to catch up to him. This turned into a run, and the run turned into a sprint, and finally, many trees later, Trevor caught up to him. "What . . . are . . ."—*huff, huff*—"you . . . doing?"

Corey spun around and faced Trevor. "You didn't need to follow me."

"Sensitivity Buddies. Ring a bell? We're supposed to be doing this together, according to Miss Plimp."

"And you always follow the rules, don't you?"

Trevor knew his truthful answer might sound slightly nerdy, but the truth was the truth. "Yes."

Corey shook his head and laughed.

A feeling welled up in Trevor, and it made his stomach ache. Why was this guy so mean to him? What had he ever done?

Corey pointed down the path. "Just search for bushes."

Trevor trudged down the trail a ways until he realized he wasn't quite sure what he was looking for. "What type of bush?"

"I dunno. Bushy and greenish. With berries. Blue ones."

Trevor took a closer look and started to remember the names of the plants and shrubs around him. Manzanita. Hollyleaf cherry bush. Sequoia gooseberry.

All that wilderness research he'd done in order to show his mom he needed out of this trip was actually starting to come in handy.

"Aha! Found it!" Corey waved him over.

Trevor approached the bush but realized quickly what Corey had found. "That's the California wild blackberry bush. *Black* is the key word there."

"Naw. They're just intensely navy."

Trevor shook his head in disbelief that they'd come all the way out into the woods for a blackberry. And now the sun was just about to drop down, which meant it would be dark soon. Only one word came to his mind: *nocturnal.* And the word *nocturnal* led to another word: *animal.*

"Let's head back. We'll grab a packet of blueberry jam from the dining hall and be done with this."

Corey slapped his forehead. "Jam! Why didn't I think of that?!"

Truthfully, Corey *had* thought of that. Pretending he hadn't thought of that was all part of his Master Plan. Corey was certain the plan was finally going to be the one that worked since he'd titled it "Master Plan: to get Trevor lost—and then find him!" Corey would become the camp hero—and the camp hero always gets the girl in the end. It couldn't fail.

Trevor took a couple of deep breaths and said, "Just lead the way. Let's go."

Trevor was close on Corey's heels, and within moments, they found themselves at a dead end facing a hollow sequoia tree.

"Other way," Corey said. He sped up his pace because "losing him" was a crucial part of the Master Plan That Cannot Fail.

Corey ran past some bushes and ducked behind a log.

So did Trevor.

Corey charged down the trail and in between a group of trees.

So did Trevor.

Corey hid behind a boulder and pretended to pick flowers.

Trevor did, too. He handed Corey a dandelion. "Are you sure this is the way?"

Corey sighed. This Master Plan That Cannot Fail seemed to be totally failing. "Let's just head back." Corey trudged down the trail.

But Trevor noticed he was going the wrong way. "We went left, not right."

"Bro. I KNOW how to get us out of here. I came to this camp last year."

"But we crossed over this trail from over there," Trevor explained.

"Fine." Corey marched back in the other direction and said over his shoulder, "Like I said, it's the other way, num-skull."

Trevor stopped and folded his arms. "You know, we're technically supposed to be giving each other compliments right now."

Corey turned around and said in a sarcastic tone, "So sorry. You are terrific at being a numskull. How's that? Now let's go."

Trevor could feel the heat rise up in his entire body, and all he wanted to do was tell Corey exactly what he was thinking. But before he could say a word, Corey spotted something.

"Check it out. I think this is the way!"

Trevor rushed up to join him but realized that what was in front of them was a tree stump. THE EXACT SAME TREE STUMP THEY HAD STARTED FROM.

Corey looked up, and shockingly, his face had lost all its color. "Dude, we are totally lost."

Trevor flopped his head, regretting that he was a rule follower. Maybe there were times when ignoring a rule was best. But no, he had followed Corey Long out into the woods simply because he didn't want to get in trouble.

Maybe Corey's right, he thought. I really am a numskull.

CHAPTER TWENTY-ONE

COREY PACED IN A CIRCLE AROUND THE TREE STUMP. "What do we do? WHAT DO WE DO?!"

Trevor remembered the first thing to do in a nature emergency was to get calm. "Stop. Sit down," he ordered.

Corey did. Then he looked up and crinkled his forehead. "Wait. Why am I listening to *you*?"

"Because if you'd put your ego aside for a second and listen to someone else rather than worry about your reflection in a mirror, then maybe this stuff wouldn't happen to you!"

"What are you so worked up about?"

"Seven minutes. That's how long you've been *somewhat* decent to me this entire school year. The rest of it, you've been trying to utterly humiliate me. You've tripped me. You made me go into the teacher's bathroom. You made me slide on mashed potatoes." Trevor shook a fist. "Why? Why, out of everyone at this school, did you have to pick on ME?"

"Because you made me feel like an idiot in front of Libby!" Corey blurted. He pushed his bangs to the side of his face, and Trevor could see that he was blushing. Corey Long—the King of Cool—was embarrassed. Corey stared at the dirt and reluctantly continued. "And you're friends with her, and she thinks you're the most interesting person on Earth or something, and I couldn't compete with that."

That's when it hit Trevor. All this—Corey being nice to him, then being mean to him—was all because of Libby. "You picked on me because I'm friends with her. You realize that doesn't make sense, right?"

"How was I going to get her to like me if all she saw was you being awesome?"

"I have no idea if you're telling the truth or if this is some sort of weird reverse psychology trick or dark magic or—"

"Look, last summer I had a swim class with Libby. She's a year younger, but she . . . she felt out of my league."

Corey shook his head, like this memory was painful. "I was too nervous to say anything to her, so I just swam as many laps as I could, hoping she'd notice me. But it seemed like every time I came up for air, she was talking to one of her friends about another guy. She would go on and on about how great and funny and awesome he was and they all needed to meet him and on and on." Corey looked away. "She was talking about you. Libby *always* talked about you."

"She was probably just trying to find me some friends before school started," Trevor said. "She's my social director, that's all."

"All I knew was there was some guy named Trevor who was practically perfect, and Libby liked him. So when I spotted you that first day, I decided to pull you down a few pegs—make sure you weren't perfect anymore."

"Which is hysterical, because the only thing I've done perfectly in life was be born on the correct due date."

"I just wanted Libby to think that maybe there were other guys out there that were cool. And making you look uncool was the only thing I could come up with. So that's why I tripped you and embarrassed you and ridiculed you on a fairly regular basis."

"*Very* regular basis."

Corey looked away and said in a low voice, "I shouldn't have followed the rules."

Trevor narrowed his eyes. "What rules?"

"The book. The one that—" Corey stopped in his tracks and stuffed his hands in his pockets. "Look, this next part is going to be embarrassing, so could you just look away for a minute?"

Trevor slowly turned and stared at a manzanita tree. "Fine. Go ahead."

"My older brother has it all figured out. He's popular and awesome and has a girlfriend, and his hair is even better than mine. I've been going to him for advice my entire life. But what do I get? Nothing. He always just says, 'Figure it out yourself, man.' So when I couldn't figure out what to say to Libby at swim class, I had only one option left. . . ."

Trevor winced. "Just be nice to her?"

"Go to the library. I found a book. . . ." Corey paused for a minute and shuddered at the thought. "It was called *The Cool Dude's Guide to Landing the Girl*." It had all these lists and rules to follow. One of the rules was to make her think you *didn't* like her—make her think you're out of her league."

"This got published?"

"So that's why I pretended to ask her to the fall dance only to get algebra answers. That idea came from page seventy-two . . . 'pretend to use her.'"

"You've written a complaint letter to the publisher, right? If not, I can draft something up—"

"So now she doesn't even give me the time of day, and it's all my fault. I gave her that note asking if she wanted to hang out at the social tonight, but she never answered. She probably doesn't even know who I am."

Trevor turned away from his manzanita tree. "Are you kidding? Libby talks about you all the time. She even made a pro-con chart about you."

Corey rushed up to him and put his hands on Trevor's shoulders. "Dude, are you serious?"

"Don't worry . . . your hair is on the 'pro' side."

He clamped down harder. "She's *actually* considering going out with me?!"

Trevor recoiled. "Wow. You really like her."

Corey stepped back, scuffing the dirt with his shoe. "Yeah, but it's cool. I'm cool. I'm relaxed. I'm cool."

Trevor smirked. Nervously repeating words . . . it was something he was all too familiar with. "Relax. Libby thinks you're cool. And trust me, you are *way* cooler than me." That was a sentence he never imagined saying out loud.

But somehow, it felt right.

With a mischievous look in his eye, Corey approached the stump and sat down next to Trevor. "You know how Miss Plimp said we are supposed to give each other compliments?"

Trevor nodded.

"Well, I'm about to give you one. But you have to look away again."

"If I have to look away, then you have to look away, too."

Corey sighed. "Fine. Back to back. Ready?"

Corey took in a bunch of air, puffed his cheeks, then blew it out up at the sky. "You may not be the most athletic or coordinated person—"

"That is technically not a compliment."

"Let me finish. And you're also afraid of stuff you shouldn't be afraid of . . ."

"Again, not a compliment."

"Just wait for it. You remind me of what I was like when I got to Westside last year. But I changed, and I thought it was a good thing—the hair, the coolness. But it's not like it got me a ton of friends. Dudes copied my haircut, but that was about it. No one started to call me and ask to hang out. Honestly, I wish I'd stayed the same." Corey's voice cracked. "I'd rather be more like you."

Whoa, Trevor thought. That is a sentence I never imagined Corey Long would say.

Trevor fiddled with a stick as he contemplated all the things he wanted to say to Corey. That Corey had been mean to him for all the wrong reasons. That he was a jerk, but sometimes he wasn't a jerk, and it made everything confusing. And that he shouldn't follow rules in a book. Maybe there are times when rules aren't good to follow.

But instead, Trevor turned around to face Corey and say just one word: *thanks*.

Except in that moment, all that came out though was, "Th . . . th . . . th . . ."

"Dude, you're stuttering."

Trevor shook his head because he wasn't stuttering at all—he was freaking out. Because just a few yards beyond Corey's shoulder was his worst nightmare.

A black bear.

And it looked hungry.

Cindy Applegate

Not feeling bouncy
at all

7:10 p.m.

This is what you would call a MEGA-DISASTER.

Even if Princess Kate rode in on a neon pink horse and asked me to move into the royal palace, my life would still be a mega-disaster.

Savannah Maxwell is not talking to me.

To. ME.

Hold on . . . gotta take care of these tears. Talk among yourselves.

[pats her eyes with tissues]

It's just that I've been so busy with my wilderness emergency, and it's all-consuming to keep Lucy happy. It's like people don't understand how hard my life can be.

And now even Lucy won't even come inside the cabin to snuggle, because she seems to like her new freedom or something. She thinks she's some sort of . . . animal.

But don't feel sorry for me . . . I'm going to take care of this problem ALL BY MYSELF. I plan to ask Marty to feed her some super fancy food tonight.

I'm a survivor.

CHAPTER
TWENTY-TWO

"**D**on't. Move." Trevor squeezed his words out of the corner of his mouth. "There's a bear behind you."

"WHAT?!"

"Shh!" Trevor covered Corey's mouth. "Be quiet," Trevor whispered.

Corey nodded. He then cut his eyes back and saw the bear sniffing around a tree. He looked over at Trevor and said in a low voice, "RUN."

But then Trevor remembered it. All his Get Out of This Trip research—there was a lot that was bear related! He clamped down on Corey's shoulder and calmly explained what was about to happen. "We will not run. That shows the bear we're vulnerable. We are going to stand our ground."

"Whoa. Dude. WHAT?"

At that moment, the bear looked up from its sniffing and noticed the boys.

Trevor took a quick breath and said, "Do what I do. Make yourself as large as possible. Don't look frightened."

Without any hesitation, Trevor stood up, making himself tall with his feet planted widely apart and his arms on his hips, superhero style. He put on his best "I'm not afraid of you" face. Strangely, doing all these things made him feel that he actually wasn't afraid. His research said to use a deep, calm voice—be in charge. "Go away, bear. This is our spot," he said.

But the bear didn't budge.

Without hesitation, Corey scooched behind Trevor, doing his best to stay unseen as he shivered with fear.

It was then that Trevor heard a sound—the familiar clanging from his ghost-in-a-band dream. The sound came from Corey's backpack.

"What's in there?" Trevor asked.

Corey quickly realized what it was . . . the tin cans he'd used for his ghost prank. All his shivering in fear had caused the cans to rattle.

"They're the cans I used to haunt your cabin." Corey dropped his head. "Sorry, man."

But Trevor's research told him the best way to scare away a bear was to make a loud sound. "Apologies later, bro. Hand me those cans!" Trevor snatched them from Corey and banged them together as he shouted, "Back off!"

The bear grunted. Then it turned and headed back down the trail. When the bear was gone, Trevor collapsed onto the tree stump. "Man, that was close."

But Corey started hopping around. "Did you SEE THAT?! We scared that bear off like a boss, bro!"

"*We* did. Sure thing, Corey." He gave him a thumbs-up. "Couldn't have done it without you."

"We gotta find our way out of here," Trevor said. But Corey was too busy doing double fist pumps in celebration of his bear scare.

It hit Trevor that it was up to him to get them back. "Follow me." Trevor marched down the trail, his head high as he used all his senses to find his way.

That's when he heard the sound of water. "Do you hear that?"

"All I hear is the sound of our AWESOMENESS!" Corey pulled another fist pump.

"Quiet. It's a river!" Trevor said.

"How will that help?"

"Remember the hike yesterday—when I humiliated

myself by being the ONLY one who didn't fall into the river?"

Corey nodded. "That was super humiliating for you, bro."

Trevor rolled his eyes. "But my humiliation might be the one thing that will save us. I can't believe I just said that."

The boys rushed through the woods in the direction of the running water. They spotted the river in a clearing and ran up to the water's edge. "There!" Trevor pointed upstream. "The bridge that I was allergic to!"

Corey threw his hands in the air. "Yes!"

With Corey on his tail, Trevor darted between bushes and trees and found the spot past the bridge where he'd easily crossed. They happily hopped from rock to rock and made it safely to the other side without even getting a drop of water on them.

Corey looked down the trail. "I see it! Dining hall lights!

"I think we can safely pull some fist pumps now," Trevor said with a smirk.

But Corey didn't pump his fists, and he didn't head down the trail back to camp. Instead, he sauntered up to Trevor. "Listen, you're the reason why we got away from that bear and found our way back. All that nature stuff that you knew . . . it was totally impressive, bro." Corey dipped his head and added in a soft voice, "I understand why Libby talks about you all the time."

"Thanks, man."

Corey poked him on the shoulder. "But I don't get it. How'd you stay so calm?"

Instantly, Trevor realized how he'd done it.

That bear.

"You know, this whole year I've been avoiding my problems. But doing that never *solved* my problems. And facing that bear head-on, standing my ground, making myself big, not being vulnerable . . ." Trevor took a deep, satisfying breath, realizing that the experience had changed him— really changed him. "It hit me that facing things head-on and not being scared . . . *that's* how you solve a problem. I guess it took me coming on this trip that I was so afraid of to realize that. And you know what? I think I'm done with being scared."

Corey's eyes grew big. "Whoa. That was deep, man."

Trevor smiled. "Let's head over to the social. I think Libby will be happy to see you back safely."

Corey bumped shoulders with him and headed down the trail by Trevor's side. "She's going to be happier to see you, bro."

Libby Gardner

Pacing nervously

7:30 p.m.

It's starting to get dark. Everyone's back from the scavenger hunt except for Trevor and Corey!

Not going to panic, not going to panic . . .

But what could be holding them up? Are they talking about me? Are they fighting? Are they lost?!

[paces and thinks out loud]

Trevor HAS to get here soon—alive and well, but mostly alive. He needs to help me fix this disaster of a social!

It took only a couple of minutes for everyone to finish the scavenger hunt because I wrote "Find something blue" on EVERYBODY'S card. I figured they'd all find different blue things, and we'd be amazed by how many blue objects we'd gathered, and it would spur on deep, meaningful conversation.

BUT NO.

All we ended up with was a heaping pile of blueberry jam packets.

208

So then the next part of the social, where they were supposed to "meander like a stream" and "act natural"?

[momentarily peeks her head inside the dining hall]

Nothing. They're doing NOTHING.

Apparently the "natural state" of a group of seventh and eighth graders is extreme boredom.

And Savannah Maxwell looks the most bored of them all. She is now counting the squares on the checkered tablecloth. But she keeps losing track and starting over.

This is a disaster.

I need Trevor back.

NOW.

CHAPTER TWENTY-THREE

HELP. THAT'S WHAT LIBBY NEEDED. AND SHE SPOTTED it in the northeast corner of the dining hall.

Molly was sitting by herself looking unusually sad, even for her. Libby rushed up to her. "Where are Trevor and Corey?"

She shrugged. "I dunno."

Libby paced back and forth in front of her. "What if they're lost? There's no way they'll find their way back. Corey probably thinks getting lost is awesome, and Trevor is, no doubt, about to hyperventilate because he's scared of the dark. He's scared of everything."

Molly threw her hands in the air. "What's the big deal? I'm sure they left footprints. They can just follow them back."

Libby perked up at that—such a simple solution. "Huh. I guess that's possible." She stopped for a moment to consider the actual likeliness of this happening.

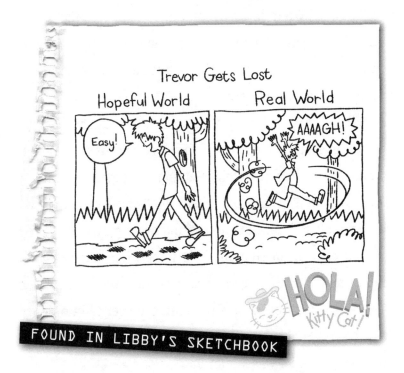

FOUND IN LIBBY'S SKETCHBOOK

Libby tightened her grip on her clipboard. "Oh, no. They're lost; I just know it. We have to tell Miss Plimp." Libby grabbed Molly by the arm and dragged her across the room with her. Molly resisted, but Libby kept up the tugging because—whether she knew it or not—Molly always seemed to come up with solutions that no one else would have thought of.

Libby tugged on Miss Plimp's sleeve. "Trevor and Corey are missing. They didn't come back from the scavenger hunt. What do we do?"

"Missing? What do we . . . um . . . gosh . . ." Miss Plimp was rattled. She had prepared for many things—games, songs, intense social interaction—but an actual emergency was not on her to-do list.

"I'll ask my dad," Molly announced. She was shocked the words came out of her mouth because she hadn't spoken to her father the entire trip. Getting a promotion wasn't a bad thing, and at one point, she had come very close to congratulating him, but the moving away part made it too hard to bear. Even though she'd hoped her three days of silence might make him change his mind about taking the promotion, she would have to break the silence in order to help Trevor. Seeing no other choice, she charged across the room to where he was standing.

"Dad, I need to talk to you."

He looked at her over his reading glasses. "I'm happy to hear that, Molly. You haven't spoken to me in days."

She leaned in closer. "It's not about the move. I'm still not talking to you about that. But right now we need you to take charge—Trevor and Corey haven't come back from the scavenger hunt. Can you help?"

Decker fumbled through his backpack. "Let's see . . . yes, I can take charge. We need to follow the procedure outlined on this incident report—"

But Molly didn't have time for things outlined on an incident report. It was just this type of attention to detail that had got him the promotion, but right now all she wanted was action. "Never mind. We need to find Trevor." Under her breath she added, "He's my only friend." Molly took off and zoomed across the room, skillfully weaving in and out of groups of students, and marched up to Marty, who was busy gnawing on a chicken wing. "Trevor and Corey are in the woods," she said to him matter-of-factly. "They may be lost. You have the survival skills to find them without an incident report. You dropped some sauce."

He dabbed at a stain on his sweatshirt. "Me?"

Libby suddenly rushed up to join them. "Yes, this is brilliant, Molly. Marty knows everything about the wilderness." She turned to Marty and put her hand on his shoulder, as if he was special . . . the chosen one. "Marty. You read all those magazines and stuff. Now go! Please! I need Trevor's help before this social ruins my reputation!"

"But—"

"GO!"

Marty nodded, ate one last bite of his chicken wing, then took off toward the woods.

On the far side of the room, there was a thunderous clang. Plates fell. Snacks spilled all over. People squealed in terror!

Everyone whirled around to see Brian and Brad Baker flailing their hands in the air. "Help!" they screamed. Then Brad, or possibly Brian (who really knows at this point!), jumped up on one of the chairs and yelled out to the crowd, "An animal! There's a wild animal in here!"

A bushy tail disappeared under a table.

The entire room screamed and howled and went totally berserk, running around trying to get away from the wild beast.

And that's when Libby's unplanned and downright boring social suddenly became very, very interesting.

CHAPTER TWENTY-FOUR

IT'S A BEAR!"

"A coyote!"

"A raccoon!"

"A WEREWOLF!"

All the kids were yelling out whatever animal came to mind, hoping they'd hit on the right one. No one knew why the first animal that came to mind for Jared Benson was a werewolf.

The only evidence they had was a bushy tail and a plate of Fancy Cheese Nips that was mysteriously missing the Fancy Cheese Nips.

Mr. Skeely stormed up to the group of kids. "Where's the animal?"

They all pointed to the far table in the corner. An

unidentified Baker twin said, "We saw it run under there. It's pretty big. And it has vicious teeth. It was possibly foaming at the mouth, too."

Libby paced the floor. *I can't believe this. A wild animal on the loose is the most exciting part of my social so far.*

But that wasn't her only problem. Trevor, who should have been at her side helping her calm down by way of emergency ranch dressing, was lost. She looked out the window, hoping to see Marty, Trevor, and Corey heroically heading their way.

But they were nowhere to be found.

Cindy Applegate bounded up to her. "What's wrong? Other than this social falling apart completely? And Savannah Maxwell still not talking to me?"

"There's a raccoon or something under the table. Which is actually good because everyone was bored out of their minds. But the worst part is Trevor and Corey are missing. Marty went to find them."

Cindy covered her mouth. She'd just told Marty to go feed Lucy, and it was a well-known fact that Lucy got super grumpy when she was hungry. And since Lucy was starting to show signs of becoming a bit *wild*, well . . . she might be more than grumpy.

But there was something about Marty choosing to

help others—even when her cat was in need—that made her feel sort of proud. In a low voice, Cindy said, "That's my Marty." She joined Libby and peeked out the window.

Skeely stepped up, excited to take control of a nature event happening right there in his dining hall. "I know how to get the animal out of here—stand back, kids."

And that's when it happened.

It.

The big it.

Skeely blew on a blow horn, hoping to annoy the wild animal out from under the table. But the loud sound scared the Baker twins, and they jumped back, tripping over each other, and Brian and/or Brad reached out to stop from falling over completely, but what he grabbed instead was the fire alarm.

The alarm rang, and shortly following that was the sprinkler system.

Soaking wet students screamed and ran to the open area just outside the dining hall doors. Libby and Cindy sprinted outside, and Libby immediately rounded up some towels to help everyone dry off. "Take this. Dry off. Everyone please remain calm," Libby instructed.

In the chaos, Cindy spotted Marty standing at the

edge of the woods with a pale face. She rushed up to him. "What's wrong?"

Marty bit at his lip. "Libby begged me to find Trevor. I'm just not sure what supplies I need. These things take preparation—"

"What are you talking about, silly?" She waved him off. "Just get out there and do what you do best—save them, Survival Man! Lucy can wait a few minutes to get her dinner."

Marty paced back and forth. "But that means I'm trying to attempt a wilderness rescue, and there's probably a checklist I should go through first."

Cindy grabbed him by the elbow to stop him. "Marty. You're the expert at all things survival-ish."

"But . . . but you don't understand—"

She narrowed her eyes. "Marty Nelson doesn't need a list from a magazine to save the world."

Marty stuffed his hands in his pockets, and his face rushed with warmth. He couldn't believe he was going to say what he was about to say. But Trevor and Corey needed to be found, and he didn't see a choice, even if it meant Cindy not liking him anymore. "Here's the thing." He kicked at a rock on the ground, then let it all out. "I know how to read a magazine, find every tip, memorize all the nature

218

facts, and I can even complete the crossword puzzle at the back without reading the clues. But the truth is, I've never even been camping. My mom is a vegetarian, and my dad is a wedding singer. The most extreme nature experience we've ever had was going for a walk in the neighborhood when there was a possibility of rain." He sighed. "It didn't even rain a drop. We are the tamest people in the world."

Marty sighed and looked away—he didn't want to see the disappointment on her face by telling her the whole truth. "I know everything there is to know about nature. . . . I'm just not certain I can go out there and actually *do* those things."

Cindy stuck her hand on her hip. "Look, that is a super sad backstory and all, but snap out of it. We have people to save! And a cat to feed!"

Marty smiled. Her yelly voice was sort of cute.

"You know what?" she said. "Something exciting *is* happening. So we're going to do this together. Hand me your magazine—there has to be something in here about tracking down a couple of middle-schoolers in the woods who are super late for a social."

He shoved it into her hands. "Page ninety-two."

Baker Twins

Explaining what
they saw

7:40 p.m.

Brian: The animal was huge.

Brad: Ginormous.

Brian: Bigger than a basketball.

Brad: No animal is the shape of a basketball—
it was more like the size of an Xbox 360.

Brian: So now the animal's the shape of a video
game console?

Brad: Whatever, you still have my pencil.

Brian: You're wearing my shirt.

CHAPTER TWENTY-FIVE

CINDY FLIPPED TO THE PAGE. "AHA! HOW TO FIND someone in the wilderness in seven easy steps!"

They headed off down the trail as Cindy read the instructions and Marty tried his best to pull together some survival-related confidence. She used her best super-positive radio announcer voice. "First, determine where the hiker was last seen. Also, there's an advertisement for a travel bed for small pets that looks *fantastic*!"

From behind them a voice said, "The hikers were last seen right here."

Cindy and Marty whirled around to see Trevor and Corey strolling up to them.

"Dude!"

"Man!"

"Bro!"

Cindy ducked out of the way and covered her eyes. "Too much guy talk, y'all!"

A group of people arrived from the direction of the dining hall.

Libby.

Miss Plimp.

Decker.

Rushing up to Trevor to put her arm around him, Libby blurted, "Are you okay? I was so worried!"

Before he could answer, Miss Plimp stepped up and clasped her hands together in a worried fashion. "What happened, boys? You can tell me anything—I'm your counselor. Was there a kidnapping involved? Anything extraterrestrial?"

Trevor paused, noticing the incident report Decker was holding in his hand. Trevor knew that the school couldn't handle one more camp incident. And Decker might be held responsible for two kids who went missing and also had to escape a bear. It could be a transferrable offense. And he couldn't stand to see Molly have to move anymore. Plus, he really wanted her to stay at Westside.

Which is why Trevor—who suffers from the disease of being always truthful—told a lie. A total, complete lie.

(His first.)

"We found some blueberries for the scavenger hunt. I ate them all on our way back; that's all that happened."

Corey tilted his head in disbelief.

Trevor continued. "But we told each other compliments, Miss Plimp." Which actually was the truth, and it made him feel a little less queasy.

With a triple clap indicating her excitement, Miss Plimp led the group back to the dining hall. But just before they reached the doors, Trevor noticed Molly standing alone by the side of the trail, her hoodie pulled tight around her head.

Libby noticed her, too, standing there looking even sadder than before. She knew this wasn't regular Bored Molly behavior. Something told her that this was much more. And even though Libby really wanted Trevor's help to get the social going again, she had a feeling that it wasn't as important as whatever Molly needed. "I'll see you inside." Libby nudged him toward Molly, then headed off to the dining hall.

"Wait, Libby!" he called after her. "You know that pro-con chart?"

She smirked. "Yeah?"

"I found out there are a lot more pros. Just thought you should know that."

Libby glanced over at Corey, who was slicking back his hair with his fingers. "Thanks, Trev. I was hoping so." She turned and joined the rest of the kids inside.

Trevor lingered on the trail and cautiously approached Molly. She was staring down at her boots.

He bent over and looked up at her. "You getting a neck ache yet? Stop looking down here."

Without hesitation, she smothered him with a hug. Then she stepped back and adjusted her hoodie. "We need to talk, Trev."

She called him Trev.

He wished that was a good sign. But something told him it was the worst kind of sign. He pointed to a log where they could sit down.

She hadn't even said a word, and his heart already felt like it was breaking.

"Sooooo, what is it that you wanted to tell me?" He really had no idea what this was going to be about, but his organs told him it wouldn't be good.

A part of him—a tiny/huge part—hoped that she would say she had a crush on him. And then another part of him—a tiny/huge part—didn't want her to say that.

Their friendship was just moving from pretty good to pretty great. What if a crush ruined all that?

Molly fidgeted with her sleeve. "I need to tell you why I've been so bummed out on this trip—more than usual. It has to do with my dad."

His face dropped. This "talk" had nothing to do with the word *crush* at all.

But then she unloaded the truth. And suddenly everything seemed related.

"My dad got a promotion. They think he's done a good job at Westside, so they're sending him to a bigger middle school to become the principal." She looked away from him and said in a soft voice, "We're moving. After the end of this week, I won't see you again."

A lump formed in his throat. He tried to respond, to say something—anything. But he couldn't.

He couldn't say a word.

Trevor Jones

In utter disbelief

7:45 p.m.

I can't believe this. SHE'S MOVING?!

I just lied to Miss Plimp to make sure he DIDN'T get transferred!

No. No, no, no. There has to be a way to fix this.

Everyone knows that the incident from last year caused Corey's brother to get in trouble, and there was a scathing newspaper article written about it. So the fact that two students got lost in the woods while on a school field trip would cause ALL sorts of bad press. So that means Vice Principal Decker would get disciplined by the school board. There is no way he'd still get that promotion!

I'm sure Molly doesn't want to move. This is the first time she's ever made a friend at a school. It's not fair that she has to leave. I can fix this.

I just have to find the guts to do it.

226

Libby Gardner

Sneaky grin

7:50 p.m.

There's one thing that didn't match up with Trevor's story. Does he realize I know he was telling a lie? I've known the guy for almost my entire life . . . of course I'm able to smell a lie from him. Not that I've had that much practice smelling his lies—which is a super weird thing to say.

My point is, I wonder what REALLY happened with Trevor and Corey in the woods. Because it certainly didn't happen the way Trevor explained. He ALWAYS eats Raspberry Zingers. Blueberry flavoring makes him feel seasick.

[lifts a brow]

The Sherlock Holmes in me wants answers.

CHAPTER TWENTY-SIX

MARTY AND CINDY RUSHED BACK TO CINDY'S CABIN to feed little Lucy a fancy dinner. With all the commotion going on in the dining hall with that wild animal and sprinkler problem, Cindy figured they'd have time to sneak away without being noticed.

"I'm sorry this isn't a true wilderness rescue," Cindy said. "It would've been a blast to find Corey and Trevor!"

Marty scratched his bald head. "Honestly, I'm more excited that Trevor had the guts to find his way back. He's pretty epic."

Cindy smiled. "Now let's get Lucy some dinner. I'm a little worried about her. She's rejecting all my attempts to fancy up her bed. She has pushed away all my ribbons. We need to talk some sense into her."

They searched outside the cabin. They looked on all sides. Under the stairs. Up the trees. But Lucy was nowhere to be found.

Cindy checked inside. She peeked under her bed. She looked under the covers. She opened drawers. But there was still no kitty in sight.

"Where is she?!" Cindy was frantic, worried that her poor kitty might be hungry and lost and tragically without a sweater.

"Let's be calm about this," Marty said. "I'm sure she didn't get far."

And that's when they heard the horrifying shrieks.

They ran out the front door and looked down toward the dining hall. Standing tall was Skeely, holding up a mangy creature drenched in water. But both Marty and Cindy knew that was no regular mangy creature in his hands.

"Lucy!" Cindy shrieked. Her white hair dye hadn't come out, even from all that water from the sprinkler.

Cindy gripped Marty's arm. "Why did she go down *there?*"

Marty thought this over for a moment, then slapped his forehead. "There was a bowl of Fancy Cheese Nips on the table. She found the *one* fancy food in this camp."

"She hunted down fancy food? Do you know what this

means?!" Cindy bounced up and down. "She still has some fancy in her! WE HAVE TO SAVE HER!"

The two of them took off in a sprint toward Skeely.

On the outside deck, Skeely lifted the creature high for all to see.

"It's okay, no need to panic," Skeely said. "I will take care of this."

Cindy rushed up to him, breathless. "That is NOT a skunk! It's my kitty . . . Lucy!" She grabbed Lucy from his arms and pulled her in close.

"Meow!"

Lucy snuggled up under Cindy's chin.

The crowd *awww*-ed.

Skeely held up a hand. "We can't have an outside animal brought onto the premises. I'll have to confiscate her."

"No, please!" Cindy yelped, tears filling her eyes.

Sensing some drama, Libby rushed up to them. "A kitty! How cute!"

Cindy grabbed Libby by the shoulders. "Help, Libby! He's going to computate her! She won't be cute without a head!!"

"He said *confiscate*—but don't worry, she won't be taken away, and she won't lose her head," Libby reassured her.

Savannah Maxwell strolled up to them. "This is all going well for you, Libby. I dared you to come up with a better party, and *this* was the best you could do? Sad." Savannah then turned to Cindy. "You. You never decorated my bed!"

Cindy bit her lip. "This isn't exactly a good time to discuss this. We are having a pet emergency. And also a party emergency."

"Wait," Libby said. "I have an idea."

Savannah crossed her arms. "That's surprising, honestly."

Libby walked over to Skeely and said, "Remember how you wanted to get the kids to follow your directions more?"

He nodded suspiciously.

"Well, letting us all keep Lucy here as a camp mascot would be the nicest thing you could do."

"You really think it will help them go through the line correctly for breakfast tomorrow?"

Libby crossed her arms and said with confidence, "Absolutely. And I have an idea that will turn this social around."

He nodded. "A camp mascot is something we could use."

She rushed back over to Cindy and said, "I need your help. Can I take Lucy with me inside to the party?"

"But she does only fancy things. Well, and wild things. She's super complicated now."

Savannah stepped up. "Don't help her, Cindy. I'm your mentor. My instinct tells me *you'll* be the class president next year."

"Please, Cindy," Libby pleaded. "We need all the decorations from your cabin. Go grab them and meet me back here!"

"No. No way," Savannah said. "Those were supposed to be for *my* bed."

Cindy marched right up under Savannah's nose and said, "Guess what? No way. All you want is for other people to do stuff for you. That doesn't make you a good class president. It makes you totally annoying."

Savannah rolled her eyes. "But Libby's not a better president."

Cindy stuck a finger in her face. "Better? Libby's the best. You have no idea how much time this girl puts into planning events. You'll *never* be in Libby's league."

Unable to think of a comeback, Savannah opted for storming off in a huff.

Cindy high-fived Libby, then took off toward the cabin and yelled back over her shoulder, "I'll grab all the decorations. I like the way you think, Libby Gardner!"

Within a few minutes, the girls had prepared a limbo game, with a twist. When trying to figure out where her social had gone wrong, Libby realized that she might not be the best at planning ahead, but she was awesome at thinking on her feet.

Libby hopped up on a chair and announced, "Okay, Westside Middle School, it's time for our first annual game of the Skunk Shimmy!"

They all looked over to find the limbo bar now covered in fancy bows and glitter and Lucy the skunk proudly standing on top. They all scrambled quickly to get in line.

There was smiling.

And laughter.

And most importantly, there was no more boredom.

Everyone was finally having a good time. This party has been saved, she thought.

It was then that Molly and Trevor came straggling in. Libby ran over to them and hugged Trevor tightly. After a moment, she stepped back and clamped down on his shoulders, giving him a stern look. "Don't ever scare me like that again!"

"Yes, ma'am."

She turned to Molly. "I'm not sure why, but I get the feeling you deserve a hug, too. Consider this a warning that I'm about to hug you, so don't get startled and possibly hurt me. Okay? So . . . here I go . . . I'm going to give you a hug, Molly. Ready?"

Remarkably, Molly didn't recoil. She didn't even flinch. What she did do was unbelievable. She grabbed Trevor and Libby and hugged them both. Together in a giant bear hug. Then she stepped back and said softly, "I'm glad you two have each other for best friends. Truly. I'm . . . happy for you." Her voice cracked, and tears welled up in her eyes.

So Molly sprinted. She sprinted past them, out the door, and up to her cabin, and then she threw herself on her bed and buried her head in her pillow.

And that's where she cried and then cried some more.

She cried like she never had before.

CHAPTER TWENTY-SEVEN

LATER IN THE EVENING, LIBBY SPOTTED TREVOR SITTING all alone at a table.

"Do you want to talk about it?"

He didn't, actually. He wanted to solve the problem—face it head-on and fix it. But strangely, it wasn't as easy as surviving a bear encounter.

Instead he looked around the room, noticing what a great job Libby had done with the party. "The Skunk Shimmy was a brilliant idea, Lib."

She smiled. "Can I tell you something?"

Uh-oh. He really didn't want any other friend "telling him something" tonight. Or ever again, actually.

"You know that *Pop Psychology* quiz I've been using with all the questions about relationship compatibility?"

"The cutting-in-line and spaghetti sauce and tooth-paste questions, sure."

"Corey failed all those what-if questions," she said. "But he passed the real-life test."

Trevor raised a brow. "Care to explain?"

"While you were talking to Molly about whatever it is that you won't tell me, I casually strolled up to Corey and told him I found a plot hole in your story—some things just didn't add up."

Trevor had had a feeling Libby might see through his story. "A plot hole? I know of no such thing." He stuck his nose in the air.

Libby suddenly turned on her Sherlock Holmes persona. And Trevor became the not-so-smart villain who often stuck his nose in the air.

Libby stuck a straw in her mouth and pretended it was Sherlock's pipe as she paced around him. "The bridge, Mr. Jones. Was that not the *exact* bridge we tried to cross on the first day of the trip?"

"It was."

"And isn't it true that the bridge in question was the one that all the students fell from due to its rickety-ness?"

Trevor held back a smile. He always liked it when Libby

cross-examined him with a fake pipe. "Indeed, I believe you are correct."

She whirled around and pointed at his jeans. "Then how did you and Corey cross said rickety bridge without getting a single drop of water on you?"

Trevor snapped his fingers. "Curses! Foiled again!" Then he added, "But we didn't actually cross the bridge, Lib. I found the easy way across. I may have found some confidence, but I'm not stupid."

She sat down next to Trevor and bumped shoulders with him. "Corey said you guys got lost. He said it was YOU who faced a bear head-on. It was YOU who located the river. And it was YOU who figured out how to get to the spot where it was easy to cross. You were a hero." She sighed a proud sigh. "My best friend, Trevor Jones, faced his fears head-on. It's a big day for me."

Trevor cleared his throat. "Look, I could say it was a big deal, but really . . . no, wait. It was a HUGE deal. I had no idea I had that in me! Honestly, you were right, Lib. I didn't need to be scared to go on this trip. Apparently, I can handle a lot more than I think."

Libby stuck a finger in the air. "By George, I think he's got it!"

"Sherlock didn't actually say that."

"I know, but 'Elementary, my dear Watson' didn't quite fit there. And technically Sherlock never said that line either, but I still like it."

Trevor smiled. "About this thing with Corey," he leaned over and whispered. "It's your call, Lib. Always was."

It was on his way back to his cabin that Trevor heard it—the sound of Molly talking to her dad.

He hid alongside the cabin and listened.

"I'm not mad at you, Dad. I was upset about moving. I can't believe I won't see Trevor anymore."

"I'm sure you two can find a way to talk and keep in touch," Decker said.

"He has Libby. What does he need me for?" There was a muffled sound as Molly blew her nose, possibly into Decker's sleeve. When she stopped blowing, he was able to make out her final words. "You're gonna make a great principal, Dad. So if we have to move to make that happen, I'm cool with that. I have my Soul Bear—I don't need anything else."

Peeking around the cabin, Trevor caught a glimpse of them walking down the dark path with Decker's arm around Molly's shoulder.

It hit Trevor, right then and there, that there was no

way he could tell the truth to keep Decker from getting that job. Decker had done a good job as vice principal and Molly was proud of him. How could he stand in the way of that?

And all of a sudden, he felt better.

He had an idea.

Wilson

Strangely flustered

8:25 a.m.

Last night was a long night. I kept waking up, thinking I heard the students' voices.

So I ended up pacing the halls late into the night trying to get back to sleep, but honestly, I just ended up counting the minutes until they got back.

I can't believe I'm saying this, but all this ME TIME has been awful. I miss their laughter and their trash, and I even miss their locker jammings. There's just something about this group of kids . . . they're special. I miss the little rascals.

So if you'll excuse me, I have to do some prep work for their arrival. I think this will be my favorite part of the entire week.

CHAPTEЯ
TWENTY-EIGHT

THE BUS RIDE BACK TO WESTSIDE MIDDLE SCHOOL was much more quiet than the ride to Whispering Pines several days before. The quietness was almost downright bizarre. It was the end of the day—there were no more classes at school. This was a good thing since the students were tired and worn out. And many were anxious to find a video game—*any* video game.

Trevor pressed his head against the bus window and peered out. As the bus pulled in, he saw there were hundreds of parents anxiously waiting for their return.

But there was only one person standing on the curb holding his own homemade sign high above his head.

Wilson.

The students spilled out of the bus and quickly loaded

up their parents with backpacks and pillows. Trevor saw his mom grinning at him from the far side of the group. In her hand was a bag of Raspberry Zingers, his favorite. He smiled back at her, grateful that his mom always seemed to know exactly what made him happy to be home.

He lifted a finger signaling that he'd be there in a moment, then pushed through the groups of exhausted students and made his way up to Wilson. "Nice sign."

Wilson folded the sign neatly. "It's strange, Trevor. I thought I was going to love three days away from you kids. But I didn't. I hated it."

Trevor smiled. "You know what else is strange? I thought I was going to hate spending three days in the woods. But I didn't. I loved it." And he had. He realized what Miss Plimp had told him earlier was true. You should trust the process.

Before he walked off, Trevor said to Wilson, "You know, my only regret is that I never got a chance to use that floor buffer of yours."

He patted Trevor on the back. "There's always next year."

"Yep. Next year."

Wilson then handed him the sign he'd made. "Keep it," he said with a wink, then walked on with a calm, cool swagger.

As Trevor watched Wilson walk off into the crowd, like some sort of janitorial wild cowboy, he realized that "next year" meant he'd be an eighth grader. And not long after that, he'd be in high school. Then college. Then working. Then doing annual taxes and complaining about it, all adult-like.

Whoa, that moment got weird, he thought.

But for now, he was glad to have one more year with Wilson.

Trevor spotted Molly standing off to the side, fastening and refastening the safety pins on her jacket. He approached her and said, "Tomorrow's the last day."

Molly rolled her eyes. "Let me do a backflip."

"Make sure you find me. I have something to give you."

She shook her head. "I don't like surprises."

"It's not a surprise, especially since I just told you about it."

"As long as it isn't a plastic snake that jumps out—"

"Nope," Trevor said.

"Or a bunch of glitter that poofs out at me—"

"No way."

"Or a zombie clown that pops out of a cake—"

"Nope. Oh, wait. I sort of love that idea."

Molly narrowed her eyes. "Just don't go overboard or anything. Got it?"

"I won't go overboard or anything. I'm guessing it probably won't even make you smile."

"You know me too well, Trevor Jones."

"See you tomorrow, then."

She sighed. "Tomorrow."

Libby Gardner

Very pleased with
herself

10:30 a.m.

The answer was easy. I didn't need Trevor to help me figure out if Corey was dating material. The answer was clear!

I just don't have time for romance right now. It's the end of the year, which means summertime, and I have so many projects planned.

Organizing my bedroom.

Reorganizing the pantry in the kitchen.

Planning my campaign for eighth grade class president.

How could I possibly have a boyfriend, too?!

So I broke it to Corey gently and told him we could just be friends. He kept swiping his hair out of his face, and I'm not sure if it was because he was sort of upset or if he was bored or if there was a fly nearby.

Anyway, it all worked out. This summer will be the best ever. And I won't even need Trevor's help. Well, except for campaign management. I will always need him for that.

[skips off]

WESTSIDE
MIDDLE SCHOOL

LAST DAY
OF SCHOOL

CHAPTER TWENTY-NINE

THE DAY WENT BY RATHER NORMALLY FOR TREVOR. ALL the teachers had worksheets for them to complete. But they were "fun!" worksheets where you got to circle things and color things and draw lines between things. One of the worksheets folded up into an elephant. It was just busywork to get through the day until the final event.

Every year on the last day of school, the students of Westside meet in the gym with their yearbooks and school T-shirts. They run around signing books and writing their names on one another's shirts with markers. Sometimes people go out of the lines and arms are written on. But no one cares.

It was the last day of school.

Everyone was excited.

Everyone but Trevor.

As strange as it sounded, he really didn't want school to be over. He was finally—*finally*—starting to feel like he belonged. Why did it have to end just when it was starting to get so good? And now these were people he wouldn't see for three months.

And there was one he wouldn't ever see again.

So that's why he showed up to school with a large grocery bag full of gifts. And the first one he pulled out was for Marty.

"Here, this is for you," Trevor said with his head barely peeking over the bag.

Marty looked down to see what was in Trevor's hand. "A journal? Why'd you give me this?"

"So you can write down your favorite survival tips. Then you don't have to carry a bunch of magazines around with you. All the good stuff will be right there."

Marty looked left. Then right. Then he did something unexpected. He hugged it.

Trevor made his way around the room. The Baker twins each got a pencil—one green, one blue—since they both kept losing them and blaming the other.

He gave Mr. Everett a new coffee mug since he seemed to

Marty, great guy

FOUND IN TREVOR'S JOURNAL

own only one. (Which made Trevor nervous about hygiene issues.) He gave Cindy a new sweater for her kitty. (Cindy almost did a backflip—in a good way.) And he gave Miss Plimp a T-shirt that he'd drawn a picture on with a marker. (As expected, she gave three excited claps.)

Miss Plimp immediately put the shirt on over hers. "Well, did you trust the process?"

He finally understood, he hoped, what she meant by that. "Facing things, not avoiding them—that was what I figured out."

She smirked. "And . . ."

"And the process it took to find that answer was pretty epic, Miss Plimp."

She cupped his chin. "You were my favorite project this year, Trevor." Miss Plimp then glided through the room, handing out compliments and enjoying her last few moments with this special group of kids.

The gift Trevor had for Corey was a little risky. But he'd put so much effort into it that he had to give it to him.

He shoved the jar into Corey's hands. "Here. It's all natural. Found the recipe on the Internet. No smell at all. You can go on any camping trip and still have perfect hair."

Corey's eyes grew big. "Wow. Thanks, man!" He immediately scooped out some goop and slid it through his hair with a graceful *whoosh*. "I don't have a mirror, but I can tell it works. Thanks, bro."

Trevor shook his hand and then said something he never thought he'd say. "I hope it works out with Libby." But he meant it. He really *did* hope it worked out.

Corey readjusted his hair, looking nervous. "She doesn't like me, man. She just wants to be friends or something like that."

Wow, Trevor thought. Didn't see that one coming.

Trevor patted Corey on the back. "Don't worry. As far as friends go, she's the best. You're a lucky guy."

Corey stood up straight, considering this. "Yeah. I guess you're right. Me and Libby as friends. That's cool."

"Later, bro," Trevor said and then sidled up next to the trash can. Before he dumped his paper bag, he snatched his one last gift, tucked it under his arm, then strode up to her.

She was sitting in the bleachers. Drawing her own pictures in her yearbook.

"Can I sign it?" Trevor sat down next to her.

Molly slid the book over to him. "You'd be the first."

He wrote out a note to her, then passed it back and waited for her response.

To Molly,
Never change.
And get ready for your
gift.
    —Trevor

FOUND IN MOLLY'S YEARBOOK

She read it, then looked up. "What gift?"

He pulled out a stack of paper. He'd printed a picture of her soul bear on the top of each sheet. "So you can draw stuff. And write letters." He poked her on the shoulder. "To me." He motioned to a sealed envelope on top of the pile. "Write me whenever you can. Every day if you want."

Molly pressed her lips together. She didn't want to tell him what she'd been thinking. But she'd thought about it all night—this speech was rehearsed well. She placed the letter back into Trevor's hands. "We can't be friends."

Trevor's stomach dropped. "What? What do you mean?"

"I've moved from school to school, always collecting

stuff like good Hello Kitty supplies or safety pins from the teacher. I don't collect friends. It's like there's something missing in my friendships, and I . . ." She looked away. "Look, they never work out. I'm sorry." She stood up and started to walk toward the door.

Trevor couldn't believe this. After all that had happened this past year, she didn't want to be friends? It was over?

He glanced up and saw Miss Plimp on the far side of the room, swaying from left to right as she proudly watched all the students signing their yearbooks. And that's when her T-shirt caught his eye. Some other kids had drawn on it with marker. And he couldn't help but notice that someone had drawn a heart around the word *Trust*.

That was it. That's what Molly has been missing all this time. "Trust me, Molly," he yelled out to her.

She turned back around, wiping a tear from her cheek.

He rushed up to her. "We're friends. And we'll stay friends. Trust me."

The final bell rang.

All the students whooped and hollered and scampered around, collecting their belongings as they hugged and squealed, saying their final good-byes.

Molly surprised Trevor. Without warning, she snatched the gift out of his hand. "Friends," she said. "I like the sound of that." Then she turned and ran out, disappearing into the crowd.

He sighed, glad that Molly had taken the Soul Bear stationery—and the sealed envelope. And hopeful what was inside that envelope would work.

But then he realized that in all his rush the previous night to get something for all these people, he'd forgotten the most important one. He rushed over to Libby. "I can't believe this—I didn't get you a gift."

She smirked at him. "You're still coming over today to help me organize my bedroom, right?"

"Yep."

"And start brainstorming campaign slogans?"

"My pen is ready."

"What more could a girl want?" She draped her arm around his shoulder and walked out with him.

He paused and looked back at the almost empty gym. Wilson was in the far corner preparing his floor buffer. He gave Wilson a thumbs-up, and Wilson nodded back at Trevor. He knew that nod. It was a nod that said, *Next year. You will use this floor buffer.*

Next year.

Trevor swallowed hard, then joined Libby and headed out the doors, leaving Westside Middle School behind them.

Soul Bear

Molly,
   Since you're going to a new school next year, you probably want some advice. I'm entirely qualified to give advice, since I've experienced every possible humiliating circumstance already. You're welcome.
   So here you go... my best advice. (Which may or may not work.)
1. Be prepared with school supplies.
2. Never forget your locker combination. If you write it on the bottom of your shoe (and I know you're a fan of drawing on weird things), then use a good marker so it doesn't rub off.
3. Always double-check to make sure you aren't walking into the teachers' bathroom.
   (See: Trevor's humiliating first day of seventh grade.)
4. "Just chill." This was Marty's advice on the first day of school and I've been trying to follow it ever since. I have a feeling I'll be trying to follow it until I'm old and gray.
5. Keep complaining. It's your signature quirk. I like it.
6. Despite what you think, smiling will NOT kill you. It may bruise your cheek muscles, but that's only if you did a smiling marathon or something. Start off slowly. One smile at a time.

smile

you (not dead)

            Your friend (always),
            Trevor Jones,
               soon to be eighth grader
               and already freaking out
               (but you knew that)

FOUND: TREVOR'S LETTER TO MOLLY

ME. SMILING HUGE. FINALLY.

FOUND IN MOLLY'S NOTEBOOK

WESTSIDE
MIDDLE SCHOOL
FINAL
INTERVIEWS

Marty Nelson

Wearing a brand-new
camouflage vest

Check it out. My parents went ahead and got me
this new vest I've been wanting. I told them all
about my attempt at almost rescuing Trevor and
Corey in the wilderness, and they were so proud,
they gave me an early birthday gift.

And get this. My parents even said they reserved
a camping space for us in the woods! They're going
to rent an RV so we'll have comfortable beds and
heating and cable TV, but STILL. I can't wait.

Yeah, it's been an all-around good year. It
will be interesting to hear how things go for
Trevor next year, when HE'S the eighth grader.

All he has to do is remember the one piece of
advice I always give: JUST CHILL.

Later, Westside.

Corey Long

Stoked to have
his hair back to
stellar condition

I'm not really sure where things will go with me and Libby. I'm heading to high school, and she'll be busy running the middle school. So for now, we agreed to meet up at the swimming pool over the summer. My plan is to beat my record number of laps and completely sweep her off her feet.

I'll keep you posted.

I have to admit, it feels pretty good to not want to humiliate Trevor anymore. It was really taking up a lot of my time.

And hey—make sure you guys edit this documentary so that I look like the hero. A superhero would be cool. You can add special effects, right? A few exploding buildings and swinging off skyscrapers through the streets of New York would be SWEET.

I'll let you guys get working on that.

So long, Westside!

Cindy Applegate

Popping a huge bubble

OH. MY. GOD. I've missed my gum soooooooo much. I plan to spend my whole summer chewing and popping my way to happiness.

Even though, honestly? I'm already pretty happy. A positive state of being, I think you call it. It's because I get to go to the mall whenever I want.

Turns out, my dad didn't get mad at me at all about sneaking Lucy onto the trip. My mom went out of town, and she forgot about Lucy, so she would've died a horrible death if I hadn't stowed her away. I mean, she would've had access to all her holiday sweaters, so it's not like she would've died being unstylish, but I'm just glad she's still with us today and that I get unlimited trips to the mall due to my mom feeling guilty.

So I'm looking forward to next year, for sure. I don't plan to run for class president—that job was made for Libby. Instead I'm going to join a

rock-climbing club. It'll impress Marty, hopefully.
But I'm only going to the club that meets at that
gym with the indoor rock wall and also happens to
have a lovely juice bar and fantastic gift shop.
Otherwise, why go?

Also? Westside ROCKS! Y'all know that, right?!

See you guys next year. I get the feeling it
will be my cutest year yet!

Toodles!

Trevor & Libby

Side-hugging

Libby: You took on a bear, Trevor.

Trevor: You put on an event without planning it.

Libby [**smiling proudly**]: We are awesome.

Trevor: Totally.

Libby: Are you worried about eighth grade?

Trevor: Me? Nah. I'm not a worrier. Are you already making plans for eighth grade student council?

Libby: Me? Nah. I'm not an Over Planner.

[glance at each other]

Libby: Let's make sure we sit next to each other on the bus next year.

Trevor: And bring each other Raspberry Zingers.

Libby: And ranch dressing.

Trevor: And never run against each other for class president.

Libby: And never enter a contest to win a school makeover on a TV show.

Trevor: And never get lost in the woods.

Libby: But always stay best friends.

Trevor: We have to, Lib. I think it's the law.

Libby [elbows him]: It was a great year, right?

Trevor [takes a deep breath]: Nope, it wasn't great . . . it was epic.

ROBIN MELLOM used to teach middle schoolers, and now she writes about them. (Any resemblance between fictional characters and her previous real-life students is purely coincidental. Probably.) She is also the author of *The Classroom: The Epic Documentary of a Not-Yet-Epic Kid*; *The Classroom: Student Council Smackdown!*; *The Classroom: Trick Out My School!*; and *Ditched: A Love Story*. She lives with her husband and son on the central coast of California.

(And don't forget to follow Robin on Twitter @robinmellom.)

Through a freak incident involving a school bus, a Labrador retriever, and twenty-four rolls of toilet paper, **STEPHEN GILPIN** knew that someday he would be an artist. He applied himself diligently, and many years later he has found himself the illustrator of around thirty children's books. He lives in Hiawatha, Kansas, with his genius wife, Angie, and a whole bunch of kids. Visit his Web site at www.sgilpin.com.